TROUBLE WITH ALICE

DONALD KEMP

TROUBLE WITH ALICE

Copyright © June 2021 Donald Kemp
Published © June 2021 Lysestrah Press

ISBN-13: 9798523003561 (paperback)

Cover Art Design By: L. B. Cover Art Designs
Formatted And Edited By: S. H. Books Editing Services

All rights reserved.

The author retains sole copyright to his contributions to this book.

No part of this publication may be reproduced, stored in a retrieval system, or transmitted in any form or by any means, electronic, mechanical, photocopying, recording, or otherwise, without prior written permission of the publisher.

For information and inquiries, please contact: **Donald Kemp**, via: don.kemp.author@gmail.com.

This book is a work of fiction and any similarities to any persons, living or dead, or places, events, or locales, is purely coincidental. The characters are productions of the author's imagination and used fictitiously.

To my editor, Nancy, and my publisher, Lysestrah Press,
for making all of this possible.

ALSO BY DONALD KEMP

I LIVE WITH A MENDED HEART
(Re-Release TBA)

RENDERING

SENIOR TOURING SOCIETY

TABLE OF CONTENTS

ACKNOWLEDGMENTS	i
CHAPTER ONE	1
CHAPTER TWO	23
CHAPTER THREE	33
CHAPTER FOUR	39
CHAPTER FIVE	45
CHAPTER SIX	57
CHAPTER SEVEN	73
CHAPTER EIGHT	79

ACKNOWLEDGMENTS

To my friends, family, and other readers, who are passionately waiting for each new book, thanks again for all of your good work.

CHAPTER ONE

BUS 86

Walking the same short distance home from the bus stop seems darker tonight. Perhaps it's the overcast sky, or she is more tired than usual. Alice wants to hurry, but she's too weary to change her pace.

She takes the two steps up to a very small landing in front of the door leading to her street-side apartment. Alice enters without looking, hanging her light blue coat on the hook, kicking off her shoes and slipping her feet into the pink bunny slippers that have been waiting for her since she left that morning.

Another day. Another night alone.

I should get a dog. Someone to wag its tail and be happy to see me. Nah, there's no place around here to take him out.

I know! A cat. Yeah, a cat. They have a litter box and don't have to go outside to do their duty.

DONALD KEMP

You can't have a cat or a dog, Alice. No pets allowed here.

Weighing almost a hundred and twenty pounds, like she did in high school, her figure is graceful and slim. Alice's auburn hair is loose around her head and face, curling several inches below her shoulders. She uses very little make-up, primarily because her paycheck doesn't allow for extra nice things.

Some say her auburn-colored eyes match her hair. Others say they're hazel, or just brown. For Alice, it doesn't matter. She's who she is. Her father died when she was twelve years old, and her mother is an alcoholic. The last time she'd had news about her, she was somewhere in Mexico. Her highest grade in school had been a C, and that had been in gym class. It wasn't because she was dumb. She wasn't motivated to learn by spending time with one aunt and then another. Sometimes, she'd spend time with a complete stranger one of the aunts knew.

At seventeen, she'd hit the streets, getting an education on how to survive from other homeless people. She'd lied about her age and went to work at a local fast food place. Two years later, she'd gotten hired by Merchants, a baby crib manufacturer.

She closes the door and sets the lock. Alice glances at the queen-sized bed to the right of where she's standing, obstructing part of the room's small window.

"Can anyone tell me why I bought a queen-sized bed? Dummy, you're all alone and those sheets cost more than a regular or twin-sized bed. It takes up more room than I have in the rest of my thirty-eight-fifty a week apartment. I've got to get a new curtain for this rod to hide things in the closet. But why bother? I don't have guests coming here."

She climbs over the bed, taking two small steps into the kitchen. Alice tugs open the fridge's door.

A cup of blueberry yogurt sits on the top shelf. Two eggs lie in a dish below, alongside half a loaf of bread. A small oleo carton is tucked into the butter compartment.

I should have stopped for a pizza or something. I have the same thought every night and never follow through with it.

Alice, you need to get a life. You're wasting your life, girl. That's what you're doing. Wasting your life. Come August, you'll be thirty-one, for gosh sakes.

"Oh, well. I'm not hungry. Just worn out and ready for bed."

She pushes the fridge's door closed and moves toward the bed. Alice falls back onto the mattress.

I should take a warm shower.

Dismissing the thought, she rolls over, grabbing hold of a corner of the blanket and wrapping it around herself before she falls asleep.

DONALD KEMP

Alice opens one eye, listening to the sound of the blaring alarm. She's intent on silencing the noise. Wrapped in the blanket, she has trouble freeing an arm to do so. She hasn't moved all night and is still wearing yesterday's clothes. She draws a deep breath and exhales, catching sight of a fly on the ceiling.

I wonder what that is like, walking upside down. Do flies ever get vertigo walking around like that?

Her thoughts are interrupted by the sound of her neighbor's doorbell ringing.

Damn, that thing is loud. Oh, well. Get up, Alice. It's time to take a shower. It's another day.

What to wear? I need a lady's maid to have things all ready for me and help me dress.

Right, when you win the lottery, dreamer.

The chill of autumn hangs in the air this morning. Alice walks up Dudley toward the corner of Third Street. The open sign in Patrick's Bakery is on. She joins another person outside the store to buy her morning snack.

The door opens. The two of them enter.

She pauses, inhaling the full aroma of the shop. The other person is greeted by one of the employees. Alice walks slowly toward the showcases and the

TROUBLE WITH ALICE

owner.

"Good morning, Alice."

"Good morning, Patrick. I'll have that chocolate covered roll in the center," she says, pointing to it.

"Good choice. One of my favorites."

He picks up the roll and places it in a bag with a picture of him and the shop's name on it.

She pays for it, says goodbye to him, and leaves the bakery, heading for Third Street with the usual morning traffic flashing by at fifty miles-an-hour in a forty mile speed limit zone.

BUS 86 is early and pulling away from the curb.

She waves her arms and runs toward it, crying, "Wait. I'm coming!"

The driver catches sight of her and stops the vehicle. He opens the door again.

"Well, hurry up. I can't hold everyone up for one person," the new driver complains.

"Where's Ted? He's the regular driver."

"How should I know? Put your dollar in the box and sit down. I've got a schedule to keep."

"I've got a transit punch card."

"Well, hand it over. There's more people waiting down the line."

I wonder what's wrong with Ted.

He punches the card and directs her to the back of the bus.

She tucks the card back in her purse and almost falls over as the bus moves forward before she can find a seat and sit down. Alice stumbles forward, struggling to find a seat due to the driver's erratic driving. She heads for the back of the bus, nodding and saying good morning to most of the passengers.

Many return her smiles and good mornings.

She arrives at her usual seat and plops down beside a woman sitting near the window. "You're new on this bus. I'm Alice. I usually sit here every morning."

The woman grunts and turns away, looking out the window.

That's the trouble with BUS 86. No one wants to talk during the next thirty minutes into town. I guess that's what we do now, ignore our neighbors.

The bus turns onto Grenade Street. Alice raises an eyebrow and sits up straight. She glances about.

Why are we going down Grenade Street? This is out of our way. Oh, well, maybe there's some construction I don't know about.

She settles back in her seat.

There's a dress shop. I didn't know that was there. I could walk this far, perhaps, on Saturday. Gives me something to do. I hope the weather is warmer.

The new driver stops the bus and rises out of his seat. "Okay, everyone, out of the bus. Come on. I don't have all day. Get off the bus."

He waves his arm at the door.

"Why are we getting off the bus?" a man asks.

"Shut up. Just get off the bus before I throw you out."

Why do we have to follow his orders? There are two big

men in front of me. Why don't they do something? No, they got off, too. Two big men and they obey like meek little lambs. I should have taken that karate class. Then, I'd wham, bam, right in his fat gut. Grandma would have stuck her hatpin in him. She wouldn't stand for this crap.

"Who are you looking at, lady? Don't stand there. Get off the bus."

"I'm memorizing your face, your clothing, and those boots with the pink laces you have on." Alice snarls. "I'll tell the city bus people and the cops everything. And that gun in your belt doesn't scare me either."

I bet that karate class would teach me how to pull the trigger while it's still in his pants and make him less of a man.

"Two big men let you do this to us without so much as a—"

The bus driver has heard enough. He yanks Alice off her feet, pushing her forward and out the door.

She trips and falls through the door, landing hard on the ground. She sits up and swears. With a flick of her hand, she plucks the broken bag with the chocolate roll in it off her coat. Alice frowns and shakes her head.

"Damn it, Fat Pig. You crushed my roll. Chocolate is all over my coat."

He laughs, turning and sliding back into the driver's seat. He pulls the bus away from the curb and continues down Grenade Street to join the speeding traffic rushing past on Fourth Street.

Her former companion is still on the bus. The

woman's eyes meet Alice's. A malicious smile spreads across her face. She waves goodbye from the rear window.

Alice looks about.

People stand nearby with blank looks on their faces. All are unsure about what to do.

"Someone should call 911. I don't have one of those travel anywhere phones," she says, standing and glaring at the two men who haven't offered her a hand.

Yeah. Someone call 911. I'll get the money someday for one of those things they call cells. I wonder why that fat pig wanted to steal a city bus.

The passengers are gathered around in several small groups, talking and wondering about what they will do. Some have left the area and are walking back to Third Street.

Now what? Wait for the police, I guess. Where can I sit down? I could walk back to that dress shop, but I'll miss the cops. I know no one else took the trouble to memorize the driver's face. I guess it's the curb.

Look at this roll, squished and chocolate on my coat. I suppose I could eat it anyway. Some of those people from the bus have walked away. I may end up being the only one here.

Those cops had better take me to work and tell Old Man Richard why I'm late. Why would anyone steal a bus, for gosh sakes? I'll ask the cops that.

Here they come. Finally!

"Hey, stop!" she cries, waving a hand in the direction of the police car.

TROUBLE WITH ALICE

They slowly drive away from her.

Alice runs beside the vehicle, shouting, "Hey, stop!"

"So, what's the matter?" the officer says, rolling down the window once the car comes to a complete stop. "I don't see anything wrong."

"A big, fat, ugly-looking man stole BUS 86 and dumped us here."

"That's the dumbest thing I ever heard. Who would want to steal a city bus? I should run you in for reporting a false 911 call."

"I didn't make the call. I don't even own a travel phone. I can tell you exactly what he looked like. Those two big men over there never even tried to object."

The officer partially rolls up the window.

"Hey, stop!" Alice yells, slapping the side of the car. "We were kicked off BUS 86, and I can't get to work now. You've got to take me to work and tell Old Man Richard why I'm late."

"Look, lady. If you persist in this story, I'll have to take you to the station. I don't see anything wrong here. The street is empty."

"If you don't believe me, ask those guys . . ." She turns around, looking up and down the street for the passengers. "Where the heck did they go? Damn those chicken-livered men. They should have stood up to that bus driver. Damn it, everyone has left."

She screams aloud with frustration, watching the police drive away. "And there go the police."

Now what? What good is a 911 call in this town if they don't believe you? I could walk back to that dress shop. Ask to use their phone. I suppose I'll have to find some room in my budget to get one of those travel phones. Everyone except me has one. The price on the ones I looked at cost more than a month's paycheck if I skipped some of the bills.

With no other option, Alice makes her way in the direction of the dress shop. It's further down the street than she'd thought. She passes an empty DYS car wash. The wind blows a paper bag down the street.

Nice apartments on the other side of the street. All the windows have the shades pulled down.

A car arrives and disappears between the apartments.

"I suppose that's where they park. Finally, here's the dress shop."

The woodwork around the large glass frame is painted in a bright green. Gold cloth drapes frame the window inside. Three slim mannequins are dressed with over-the-shoulder dresses. Two are wearing very short skirts that have slits along the side of the legs. The third mannequin has a dress on that is a few inches above the knees.

Alice glances at one of the price tags that are visible. Eight hundred dollars is listed upon it in tiny letters stating, 'sale price.'

Heck, I can't afford this neighborhood.

Alice curls her fingers around the door handle. She wiggles it. It's locked.

TROUBLE WITH ALICE

"Now what? Oh, a sign. 'Open twelve to six, Monday through Friday.'"

Scratch this shop off my list. I work all week. And who is fooling who? I can't afford it.

A soft sigh escapes her. She continues down the street and makes her way back to Third Street, ignoring the beauty shop and some sort of tobacco and pipe shop.

A bus idles at the corner stop.

"Wow. Lucky me. No waiting." She approaches and boards the bus. "Did you hear about your hijacked bus this morning?"

"No. Put your dollar in the slot on the fare box and move on."

"I already paid for today. Here's my card. See, it's punched for Tuesday morning."

"Yep. It's punched. When you get off, and then want back on, it's another dollar. Just put your dollar in the fare box, lady."

"Hey, lady, move it!" a waiting passenger behind her yells.

"If you don't put your dollar in the fare box, you'll have to get off the bus," the driver repeats.

Alice opens her purse and fumbles for a dollar. She slips it into the box.

"There. It's in the slot. I better get this back."

She hurries down the aisle, finding an empty seat by a window and sitting down.

DONALD KEMP

Alice's boss, Mr. Richards, is sitting at his desk. She knocks on his door.

He motions to her through the glass window to come into his office. The very small room has a desk and an office chair. A filing cabinet is tucked against the wall. Two small straight back wooden chairs stand in front of the desk. Several papers are stapled across a wall.

She enters his office.

He points to the chairs.

She sits down on one, having difficulty squeezing in because the chair is so close to the wall and his desk.

Mr. Richards fusses with several papers. Minutes pass before he looks at her.

"Okay, Alice. Why are you almost an hour late?"

"Sorry I'm late, Mr. Richards. The bus was hijacked and went down Grenade Street. We all had to get off. Someone called 911, and when the police came, I was the only one left to tell them what happened. They didn't believe me and drove away, leaving me half a mile from Third Street. I had to climb that steep hill on the west side of the overpass to catch another bus."

A dubious look spreads across his face.

"That is some story, Alice. The best one I've heard in all the time I've been here. I'll let it go this time, but if you're late again, no dice. I'll have to dock your pay. Don't forget, three times late, and you're fired. You have two piles of folders on your desk and

TROUBLE WITH ALICE

more on the floor already. You better skip lunch and get caught up."

"I forgot to get pizza again. I guess I should call the police and report what I know about that ugly, fat pig that pushed us off BUS 86."

Alice stacks the two pillows against the headboard and plops down on the bed, resting her head and shoulders upon them. She grabs the telephone and dials the number for the police she keeps on a pad beside the phone.

"Hello, Desk Sergeant Jones, may I help you?"

"Hello. Who do I talk to about BUS 86 that was hijacked this morning?"

"What hijacking? We don't have a report of a bus being hijacked. Who are you, lady?"

"My name is Alice Grey. I have important information along with a description of the guy that took BUS 86."

"I don't have a report about a missing bus," he repeats.

"Well, someone from BUS 86 called 911after we had to get off, but everyone left before the cops came. They wouldn't believe me, threatened to arrest me, and take me to the station. So, what good is 911 if they don't believe a person?"

The mouthpiece crackles. Officer Jones speaks to someone nearby.

"Take this crank, Tobin. Some woman wants to report a missing city bus. She says it was hijacked this morning."

Static echoes on the line. Tobin grunts.

"I would like to just once come to this shared desk and find room for me to work. I should leave those papers on the floor."

Papers crinkle in the background. The phone crackles once more.

"Hello. I'm Officer Tobin. Who is this?"

Geez, another cop. Do I have to report my info a hundred times?

"I'm Alice Grey. I've important information and a description of the fat pig that hijacked BUS 86."

"You need to come down to the station to file a report. We can't take them over the phone. Too many crank calls. I don't see anything on the docket about a hijacked city bus. Why don't you call the bus company?"

"They close at five and you get a computer asking you to press buttons. Why not check the 911 records for the call around seven-thirty?"

"I'm sorry, but we can't do that without a report."

"That's what I'm trying to do."

"Like I said, lady, we can't take a report over the phone. You have to come down to the station and file a formal report." The receiver crackles. He speaks to his companion. "Do you have anything about a bus hijacking?"

"Not a thing. She's just another crackpot."

His attention returns to Alice. "We don't have anything about a missing bus. If you come down to the station, we can take your information."

"I work all week and can't take any time off to come to your station."

"Is there anything else I can help you with, ma'am?"

Sitting up, one of the pillows falls to the floor. She looks at it and kicks it across the room, upset about the run-around she is getting.

"Well, when you get a report about a missing city bus, I'll see if I can fit you into my demanding schedule."

"I don't work this Saturday, ma'am."

"Well, then, I guess you'll never get my report. GOODBYE!"

She slams the receiver down. Alice rolls off the bed and pulls off her clothes, heading for the bathroom. She tosses the garments she's taken off in the direction of the dirty clothes basket. Most miss the mark and fall to the floor. She stares at the unintended mess and sneers.

"And I'll pick you up tomorrow." She enters the bathroom and closes the door. "Now why do I close the door? There's no one else here. What a silly thing to do. Maybe I should take the damn thing off the hinges and give it to the super. I wonder what he would say to that."

The phone rings in the other room.

Let the machine answer the phone, Alice. Take your shower.

She reaches into the shower stall and turns the hot and cold taps on, intent on making an adjustment to a comfortable temperature. Once satisfied, she steps inside.

Water feels so good. I could stay here for an hour. Ya, and pay the hot water heater bill, too.

Several minutes later, she finishes her shower and steps out, wrapping the bath towel around her and curling another towel around her hair.

Oh, well, time to find something to eat.

She leaves the bathroom and walks eight steps in her bare feet to the kitchen, rubbing the towel across her wet hair to dry it. Alice grabs the fridge's handle and tugs the door open. The cup of blueberry yogurt is still on the top shelf.

"I've two eggs from last week. I could make some French toast."

She grabs the eggs and places them on the counter before turning around and reaching for the bread. A soft sigh escapes her.

What? Rye bread for French toast? Who would know the difference? I guess bread is bread.

"Someday, I'm going to stop for a pizza. Hell, I say that every night. Call them and ask for delivery. Right, delivery, and who around here would pay for that? Plus the tip?"

TROUBLE WITH ALICE

She closes the refrigerator and turns toward the counter. Alice prepares and cooks the French toast, taking the plate with her into the bedroom-living room. She sets it on the small, round table near the TV, flopping down on the sofa. A TV Guide lies on the floor nearby. She grabs the remote and turns on the television, randomly flipping through the channels.

As usual, nothing on TV tonight. I should go to bed.

She turns it off, finishes her French toast, and stands, walking toward the sink with the dirty plate. The phone rings once more, causing her to stop in her tracks.

"So, do I answer the phone, or let the machine do it? Hell, it's on the way to the bed. I'll get it."

She grabs the receiver and balances the dirty plate in one hand before taking three short steps to the kitchen. Alice sets the plate on the counter. Grabbing a towel curled around the handles of a kitchen drawer, she wipes her hand and the telephone.

"Hello."

"Are you Alice Grey?"

"What do you want? Who are you?"

"I'm Officer Tobin from the police department. You talked to me before. You wanted to tell us something about the city bus that's missing."

"Do you know it's after ten o'clock? Why are you calling me so late? I don't have time to tell you anything right now. Call me on a Saturday. Right now,

DONALD KEMP

I have to go to bed. I work tomorrow and can't be late again or they will fire me."

"I don't work this Saturday. You can come down to the station, and someone else will take your report."

Alice is now a step away from the bed. She pulls the cover aside and sits down on its edge.

"I'm not coming down to your station. I tried to give you the information on the phone once before, and you refused. I tried to tell the police that answered the 911 call, and they drove away. Now you want me to adjust my time and spend money to come to see you, while I'm spending half the night talking. I have to work in the morning. Well, it's not going to happen, Mr. Tobin. GOODBYE!"

Disgusted, Alice drops the receiver onto its cradle. She leans back and moves to the center of the bed.

The phone rings again.

"Phooey. Let the machine get it. Phooey with PJ's. I'm going to bed as is."

The answering machine echoes in the distance.

"Hello. This is Officer Tobin. I would like to make an appointment for ten o'clock with an officer on Saturday. Please return my call. The number is five-five-five-nine-eight-seven-six."

"Well, maybe, Mr. Tobin, and maybe not. You guys had two chances to get my information and turned me down. Now, you can just wait. I'm going to sleep."

TROUBLE WITH ALICE

"Is that my alarm already? I just got to sleep." She glances at the clothes scattered around the basket nearby. "Well, so what if I missed some of them? *Almost all of them, Alice.* So what? All dirty from work yesterday. I don't know why I had to dust the file cabinets and wash the floors in the basement. Don't I get a few perks for almost ten years working there? When I get to work today, I'm going right up to that Richard guy and telling him . . ."

The sound of the phone ringing catches her attention.

"Is that my phone ringing again? I don't get calls for two weeks, and now three in two days. Oh, well, get out of bed and answer the phone. I wonder who would be calling this early."

She rests a moment on the edge of the bed and gathers her thoughts. Alice reaches for the phone.

With a sleepy voice, she says, "Hello."

"This is Officer Harris. I tried to call you last night, but got your machine. I need you to come down to the station for your report about that bus thing from the other day."

"How many times do I have to say it? I can't come down to the station during the week because I work and can't take time off. I'm not going to spend money for the bus I must take to be there on Saturday, or any other day, then find out you're not there. Got it?"

"When can I meet you?"

"Sometimes, on Saturday mornings, I go to the laundromat on Third Street. I don't know if I'll be there this Saturday. I may not have enough clothes to wash by then. It's a long walk up the hill pulling my cart."

Alice struggles to hold onto the phone, intent on getting dressed at the same time. The receiver slips out of her grasp and clatters to the floor.

She slides her arm into the other sleeve of her blouse and mutters, "Damn it."

Bending forward, she grabs the receiver and straightens, holding it to her ear.

"Did you say something? I missed it."

"I said, damn it, and I don't know when I'll be at the laundry. Goodbye." Slamming the phone down onto the cradle, she sneers in disgust at it and finishes getting dressed. "I think I'll skip breakfast today. Perhaps, I'll get two rolls at Patrick's Bakery and eat one at the bus stop. I'll save one for the morning break. I hope Ted is back."

Alice grabs the rest of her belongings, sets the lock, and slams the front door closed behind her. Walking the short distance to the bakery, she enters and discovers she's the only customer there today. She approaches the counter and is greeted by Patrick.

He claps his hands together. Flour bursts into the air.

"Good morning, Patrick. I think I'm going to have two chocolate rolls today. I'll eat one on the bus, and one at break time."

TROUBLE WITH ALICE

"Two chocolate rolls coming up," he announces with a wave of his arm.

Alice pays for her two rolls and leaves the shop. She resumes the short walk to the bus stop. Upon arriving, she recognizes most of the other passengers and exchanges greetings with a few of them.

A different bus arrives to continue the route for BUS 86.

Alice is the first in line. She boards the bus and pauses on the first step, noticing another new driver.

"Who are you? Where is Ted?"

"He's still in the hospital from the beating the other day when they took his bus. I'm Walt. Get on board."

"Beating? Ted took a beating when those guys stole our bus? How is he?" Turning to face the other passengers, she says, "Ted got beat up when they stole our bus and is in the hospital. We should all go there and wish him well."

"Would you people please get on the bus?"

"We will need some official ID after yesterday's mess and Ted's getting hurt."

"Of course. Right there, inside the door in that plastic frame. Walter McCarl, at your service. Step aboard."

Alice leans into the doorway, looking at the frame where Walter has his picture ID. She decides he is legitimate and steps into the bus.

"Okay, this guy is legit. We can board the bus," she says to the people behind her.

She holds out her transit card.

Walter punches it.

"When will Ted be back?" she asks, retrieving the card and putting it back in her purse.

"We don't know. Please take a seat. There are others behind you that want to board."

She nods and heads down the aisle, taking the window seat at the back of the bus where she usually sits. Thoughts of poor Ted in the hospital rush through her head.

I wonder if a missing bus made the news report. I'll pick up a paper from the newsstand next to the office.

CHAPTER TWO

ALICE VERSUS DETECTIVE HARRIS

Instinct senses danger. Alice stops putting clothes in the washer. She looks up, catching sight of a strange man heading in her direction.

His eyes are firmly fixed on her.

Without looking, she reaches under the pile of clothes for the rolling pin she keeps in the basket for protection.

Ah, there it is. Good thing I put this in here now that I don't bake much anymore. One more step, Mister, and you get it.

"I need whatever info you have about the missing bus," the man blurts out.

"Who the hell are you, and who are you looking for? Don't come one step closer!"

DONALD KEMP

This jerk better step back, or he gets it right in the kisser.

Alice backs away, the rolling pin hidden behind her back, moving closer to the front of the shop. Her eyes are focused on the man.

He rummages through his shirt pocket for his logbook, looking up before moving toward her. "Are you Alice Grey?"

"None of your damned business."

Her fingers curl around the rolling pin's handle. Alice raises her arm, adopting a battle stance. She's ready for him should he take another step.

"Officer Tobin says you may have some info about BUS 86."

"You were supposed to make an appointment. You got any ID?"

He opens his jacket enough for her to see the badge fastened to his belt.

Alice catches sight of a gun in a holster.

"So what can you tell us?" he asks.

"I don't see a name. What else do you have?"

He's a tad startled by her request. Nevertheless, he reaches into the pocket near his gun.

Alice panics, unsure if he's going for the gun. She swings the rolling pin in a vicious arc, striking his arm. The pencil stub and logbook fall to the floor.

He steps back and screams in pain.

She lifts her arms once more and moves toward him.

This time, he's ready and backs away.

Alice's swing misses.

TROUBLE WITH ALICE

With his good arm, he grabs her wrist and spins her around, pinning her against his chest. "Damn it, lady, stop. I'm a policeman. Drop that damned rolling pin. I think you broke my arm. Drop it!"

Alice squirms within his grasp, intent on freeing herself. He is too strong and holds her tight.

A woman rushes to her aid. "Throw it to me, Alice. I'll hit him again."

She struggles to do as the woman asks.

His grip on her arms tightens. The rolling pin clatters to the floor near her feet.

He turns, putting enough distance between himself, the rolling pin, and the approaching lady, dragging Alice with him.

"Stop right there, lady. I'm a cop. Stop!"

She hesitates, though she's hell-bent on helping Alice. The woman drops to her hands and knees, reaching for the rolling pin.

Desperate, he kicks out. His foot connects with the middle of her body.

She screams and rolls across the floor in pain.

"Now, listen, you two. I am a cop. This has got to stop before anyone gets hurt. My name is Detective Harris." Recovering his hold on Alice, he asks, "Are you going to sit on the floor beside this other lady, Miss Grey? I'll let you go if you sit down right away."

Alice doesn't say a word. She frowns, searching for a way to slip out of his grasp.

"Are you going to sit?" Harris demands.

She isn't ready to give up. Alice remembers a TV show where the victim stomps on the attacker's foot. She can't move very far, since he's holding her so tight. Nevertheless, she raises her leg and jams her heel down on his foot.

He cries out with alarm. His grip slackens.

Alice breaks free. She spins away, kicking the rolling pin in front of her.

"Damn it, woman. Calm down. I'm a cop."

"Hit the pervert again, Alice," her friend yells. "He kicked me. Hit him once for me."

She picks up the rolling pin and swings it at Harris.

He is ready and avoids her attempt, hitting her square on the jaw with his fist clenched tight, knocking her to the floor. He follows her down, flipping her onto her stomach. A knee pressed against the small of her back allows him to grab his cuffs and snap them around one of her wrists. He jerks her arm against her back and secures it with his knee, reaching for her other arm, pulling it close enough to snap on the remaining cuff.

"Now, you stay there a minute, and don't move a muscle. Hey, you!" he cries, motioning to the man hiding behind one of the machines. "Don't stand there. Call the police."

TROUBLE WITH ALICE

Several police cars have arrived.

An EMS medical truck follows a short distance behind.

People rush out of the laundromat, some heading for their cars in the parking lot. Several people mill about, talking to each other about what has happened inside the shop.

An hour later, Alice's friend has been sent to the hospital for possible treatment from the kick she's received.

Harris has an ice pack wrapped around his sore arm. The medics have determined there is no damage to his stomped foot, but it will be sore for a few days. He limps around, talking to other officers, while making a verbal report to his captain.

Still restrained, Alice sits on the tailgate of the EMS truck. She has finally accepted that Harris is a cop.

The medics want her to go to the hospital. A cold pack is pressed against her jaw.

She shakes her head, refusing medical treatment.

Harris approaches her. "I guess I should have showed you my badge and introduced myself better in the beginning, Miss Grey. I'm sorry about your jaw. Don't you think we should take you to the hospital and have them make sure it's not broken?"

Alice mumbles. The pain in her jaw prevents her from speaking properly. The bandages wrapped around her head hold the cold pack in place.

"After that bus thing the other day, I guess I'm a

bit touchy," she says, shaking her head once more.

Harris nods at an officer standing nearby. "You can take her cuffs off now."

"Are you sure, Detective?"

"Alice?"

"Yeah, there's too many of you here now to win a fight."

The officer nods and approaches her. In the blink of an eye, he unlocks them and slips the cuffs off her wrists.

"You do put up a mean fight, Miss Alice Grey. Are you ready to tell me about the hijacking now?" Harris asks.

"So, you guys finally admit there is a city bus missing, and now you think I'll tell you about everything I saw?"

"I hope so. It's missing alright. We didn't get the report from the city until late yesterday. Tobin called you a few minutes later and tried to get any info you had."

"Yeah, he calls me after ten o'clock, when I'm on my way to bed, and says I should come down to the station to make a report. I can't spend money to do that. How come no one wanted to talk to me before?"

"I regret your difficultly. And I do extend apologies for treating you badly."

"Well, I suppose I can give you what information I know. You'll have to come back inside the laundromat. I have to get my clothes washed and back to my apartment before dark. If you want more info, you'll have to follow me."

Harris nods and follows her inside, leaning against one of the machines near her.

Alice rubs her jaw. She adjusts the cold pack so she can speak better.

"Look at these bruises on my arms. You did that."

"Sorry, but I had to restrain you before we hurt each other anymore than we did."

She sighs and turns to the washing machine. She drops her clothes inside and puts in three quarters. She's missing one, unfortunately. Digging through her pockets, she's unable to find another quarter.

"I need one more quarter. Can I borrow a quarter from you?"

Harris rummages through his pockets and discovers he has a pocket full of change. He takes them all out and holds his hand toward Alice.

"Here, take what you need."

Alice takes several quarters, putting one in the machine and slipping the rest into her pocket. "I may have a second load and need more quarters," she says, glancing at him.

Harris taps his foot against the floor, patiently waiting for her to talk about what she'd observed. "Anything else before you tell me your information?"

She looks at him and makes him wait a few minutes before slowly walking to one of the chairs nearby. Alice sits down. She pauses, brushing imaginary dust off her slacks and running her fingers through her hair.

Harris pushes himself off the machine. He moves toward her and drops onto the chair next to Alice, shifting it around so that it faces her.

"Well, talk."

She notices he doesn't have a pencil and paper. "Aren't you going to write this down?"

"I'm good at taking notes in my head."

"Don't come around later and want me to repeat myself. Are you ready?"

"Yes, ma'am."

"The driver that pushed me down was very fat and a bit taller than me. I'm five-foot-three, so he would be about five-foot-six or so. He had brownish hair, one brown eye, and one blue, or perhaps hazel. The woman had two feathers in her hat, one red and one blue. I couldn't tell how tall because I only saw her sitting."

"A woman? How do you know she was with him?"

"She was smiling like that cat in Alice in Wonderland. She waved to us as the bus drove away. I tried to talk to her on the bus, but she ignored me."

"A woman, eh? That's a new lead. What did she look like?"

"I can't tell you much, but she had a very short black skirt on, and those new six or seven inch spiked shoes. Her nails had that glow in the dark sparkle stuff on them. That's about all I can tell you about her. Oh, wait, dyed hair. Looked like a bluish tint of some kind."

"You have been very helpful, err . . . Miss . . ."

"I thought you had a good memory? Now you can't even remember my name?"

"I'm sorry, ma'am. I guess the shock of you mentioning a woman sort of got to me."

"Did I tell you about the fat pig's pink shoelaces? He was a white dude about forty or fifty, or maybe sixty. What kind of man wears pink shoelaces at that age?"

"That is kind of weird, but it also means we can spot him and take action. Thank you for the information, ma'am." Harris tips his cap. "I guess I'll bum a ride to the hospital and get this arm looked at. I hope they don't have to put a cast on it. Maybe just a lightweight brace for a while."

He stands and limps to the door.

Alice moves toward the window. She catches sight of Harris slipping into one of the squad cars. It pulls away from the curb, seconds later.

Waiting for the washer to finish, she watches traffic pass by, sorry about the fact that she hit Harris with the rolling pin.

Why didn't he stop when I asked him to? None of this would have happened.

The washer clicks in the distance. She waits while the spin cycle slows down and finally stops.

"Oh, me. Get up, Alice, and dry your clothes. You have to stop at the grocery store on the way home. Damn, this jaw hurts. He really clobbered me."

CHAPTER THREE

THE PLOT

"Where is everyone? Hello, anyone here? I've got the bus," Buster says, leaning out of the driver's side window and honking the horn.

"No horn, you stupid idiot," the woman cries. "Do you want everyone in the neighborhood to come out and see this bus?"

"Hold your horses. I'm coming," a man standing near a small entrance door that's open yells.

He pauses, glancing up and down the alley to check that no one else is nearby. Satisfied it's empty and the bus they've been waiting for, he presses a button on the wall. The garage's double doors open slowly.

Buster drives the vehicle inside.

"Follow me," the woman says once it comes to a

complete stop.

She stands and rushes out of the bus, walking toward the rear of the garage and yelling at the man who'd opened the main doors. "Hey, you dope. Close the doors. Do you want everyone in the city seeing this bus?"

"Where are we going?" Buster asks, hopping off the bus and falling in behind her.

Her high heels click-clack across the cement floor.

Buster follows her, his eyes focused on her swaying hips. He tries to imitate her actions, but fails and almost trips over his own feet.

"Back to the air conditioned room. Nobody wants to sit out here in this hot, dirty garage waiting for you to show up."

"Here we are, Little Mack," Irene says, opening a door at the rear of the garage and entering a small office. "One city bus."

She slumps down onto a plush cushioned chair.

"Any trouble?" Little Mack asks, sitting behind a mahogany desk in an overstuffed office chair.

"No trouble. No mess. Everything came down, smooth as silk," she says.

"I pushed a lady out the door, and she fell on her chocolate éclair. You should have been there. Splat, all over her coat," Buster says, and laughs.

"Irene, I thought you said there was no trouble."

"I didn't think that was any trouble. She wasn't hurt, just a little chocolate on her coat. When Buster stood up and ordered everyone off the bus, they marched out like kindergarteners playing follow the leader."

"Okay, let's go over the plan."

Little Mack stands and walks over to a large round table in the center of the room.

Buster, Irene, and two other men gather around him.

He sets a city street map on the table with red lines drawn on several streets, leading to a Metro Bank and back to the garage. "Okay, listen, one more time. First, Buster drives the bus to this empty space behind the bank. Irene takes the Buick to the lot behind Food Store on Fifth Street. Pete and Jose, you are with me. We go into the bank. Jose, you stand near the guard, and when I yell, 'This is a hold-up. Everybody on the floor,' you make sure the guard goes down and take his gun."

"What if he doesn't lie down?" Jose asks.

"I told you before. Hit him over the head."

"With what?"

"What did you do with that sack of quarters I gave you?"

"I put most of them in the candy machine. Want some gum drops?"

Sighing loudly, Little Mack presses a hand against his forehead, leaning over the table. A moment passes before he rises.

Irene struggles to keep herself from laughing. She tilts her head to one side, away from Little Mack.

Pressing his face close to Jose's, he yells, "You idiot! I told you to keep them for the bank robbery."

"I saved a few. Why are you so mad? Do you want them back?"

"Irene, you can stop laughing. Go get some more quarters from the Chinaman next door."

She laughs quietly and leans forward. With both hands, she pretends to pull the flowered hose on both of her legs up. Her short skirt reveals a good portion of her flesh, drawing the men's attention.

She stands, and says, "If he asks, should I tell him why we need them?"

"Go!" Little Mack screams.

Buster takes a few steps away from the table, humming a faint tune.

"Where are you going, Buster?"

He stops walking and turns around. "Going to the head," he says, pointing to a door.

Pete drops onto a chair, examining a racing spreadsheet.

Jose sits down beside him.

Little Mack wraps both hands around his head. Eyes wide open, he glares at the ceiling, raising his arms.

"Why me? Why do I get all the idiots? Is it too much to ask for a few dollars? I'm not greedy. Just a few dollars." He pulls a chair to the table, sits down, drops his head onto his arms, and moans. "Why me?

TROUBLE WITH ALICE

Little Mack and his crew are gathered around the round table again.

Buster leans across the map.

"Get your damn elbows off the map. One last time. Park the bus here on the side of the bank. Did you hear that? Park the bus behind the bank."

"Yes, Boss. Behind the bank."

"Irene, take the Buick to the parking lot at Food Store. Pete and Jose, you come into the bank with me. Jose, go stand near the guard. When I yell, 'This is a hold-up. Everybody on the floor,' you make sure the guard does, too. If he doesn't, hit him over the head with the sack of quarters. Take his gun. Everyone got it so far? Okay, Pete, you come to the teller's windows with me. I'll take one, and you, the other."

Everyone nods, except Pete, whose nose is buried in his racing spread. He's intent on picking a winning horse for tomorrow's race.

Little Mack stares at each of them, looking for a sign that might ruin his hold-up plans at the bank.

"What if there is a line?" Pete asks without looking up.

"We cut in. Besides, they should be on the floor. You say, 'Give me all the cash in your drawer.' We take the cash, walk out the back door, and get on the bus. Buster drives us away, and we meet Irene at the Food Store. We leave the bus in the parking lot. We all get in the Buick and come back here to the garage. Now, any questions?"

Buster raises his hand.

"Yes, Buster, what is it?"
"Can I go to the head now?"

CHAPTER FOUR

ALICE SAVES THE DAY

Little Mack, Jose, and Pete are standing near the front entrance of the bank, going over the plans again.

"Remember, Jose, you stand behind the guard. If he doesn't drop to the floor when I yell, 'This is a robbery,' what do you do?"

"I hit him with a roll of quarters."

"Perfect. Where are the quarters?"

Jose rummages through one pocket and then another. He finds the roll of quarters, pulling it free and holding it aloft.

"Here they are, Boss."

"Don't put them back in your pocket. Hold them in your hand."

"Yes, Boss, in my hand. Which one?"

"Your right hand. Okay, put on your masks, and

we'll go in."

Jose puts the quarters in his pocket so he can put on his mask. They enter the bank.

"Which one is the guard?" he whispers.

"The one in the blue uniform. Just walk over there, very casual-like, and try to get behind him." Little Mack turns to Pete. "Get ready to go to the teller's window and order her to give you all the cash."

Before Jose can get behind the guard, Little Mack yells, "This is a hold-up. Everybody on the floor."

Several customers turn in his direction. Their eyes widen, though none of them drop to the floor.

"I'm not getting on the floor. I just washed these clothes," Alice says. "Look, Stupid! Your partner is fighting with our guard."

Little Mack turns around.

Alice lunges at him and tackles him to the floor.

He bumps his head hard and shrieks in pain.

She grabs the arm of a man standing nearby and pulls him down on top of Little Mack.

"Hold him down. I can't do it alone."

One of the tellers pushes the silent alarm for the police.

Two men decide to help Alice.

The first man pins Little Mack to the floor.

Pete stands to one side, watching the scene unfold. He decides to leave, taking off his mask and calmly walking out the front door.

Jose and the guard are now wrestling across the

floor.

The guard struggles to pull out his gun.

Jose struggles to grasp the roll of quarters in his pocket. Neither succeeds in achieving their goals.

"Let's rest a moment," Jose pleads. "I'm getting tired."

He pulls the mask off his face, wiping his brow. He and the guard sit up.

"Are you trying to rob the bank?"

"No." He pulls the roll of quarters out of his pocket. "I'm supposed to hit you on the head with these quarters. Little Mack and Pete are holding up the bank."

"I think I saw someone take off a mask and walk out the door."

"That must have been Pete. Little Mack is under those people, who are holding him down on the floor."

Sirens echo in the distance. The police have arrived. Several officers rush into the bank with their guns drawn.

"Over here," Alice cries. "We've got the ringleader pinned down."

Officer Tobin approaches her, eyeing the three men holding Little Mack down. "Okay, folks. I'll take it from here."

Two people whisper amongst themselves.

Soon, everyone is talking aloud. Several surround Alice, patting her on the back for helping to capture one of the bank robbers and stopping the hold-up.

Tobin glances at Alice. He then turns his attention back to Little Mack.

"Anyone else in on this hold-up besides you?"

Little Mack raises his head. He looks about, searching for Pete. To his dismay, he is long gone. He catches sight of Jose sitting next to the guard.

"He is. That man over there."

"You mean the guard was in on this?"

"No, the other one."

Tobin motions to several officers standing nearby. "Cuff them both. We'll figure out who is who at the station. I'll start taking statements from these customers. You first, ma'am. What on earth made you jump on that man?"

Alice blushes. She tucks her chin against her chest.

"He wanted me to get on the dirty floor. I just washed my dress. I told him so. And then he walked toward me, so I told him to look at the fight going on with the guard and one of his henchmen. I jumped on him when he wasn't looking."

"That's about it, Officer. Then, I jumped on him, too," a man says.

"Actually, I pulled him down, Officer."

"Well, I was about to help you."

TROUBLE WITH ALICE

"About that time two other men sat on him, too," Alice adds. "Can we get back in line now? I have to cash my paycheck and get home before dark for a change."

"I guess so, if the tellers will take you," Officer Tobin says.

"Why wouldn't they? The robbery is over. Let's get back in line. I need the cash."

CHAPTER FIVE

FIRED

The sight of a large crowd gathered around the time clock greets Alice from the moment she steps through the employee's door.

Everyone clutches documents in their hands, waving them in the air and talking loudly.

"Why is everyone so excited?" Alice asks.

"We're all getting pink slips."

"You mean we're fired?"

"That's right. The company is folding, and we get nothing."

"Well, isn't that a kick in the rear?"

So, now what? I'll have to move. I can hardly make the rent as it is. I wonder if Carl still has that old camping trailer. Maybe he could loan it to me until I find another job.

Alice unlocks the door to her apartment and steps inside. She's not sure what she'll do now that she no longer has a job. She decides to call her friend, Carl.

He answers on the first ring.

"Carl, this is Alice. How are you doing?"

"Alice? We haven't talked for a month of ages. Not too bad. And you?"

"I got fired today."

"Fired? What for?"

"Everyone got a pink slip because Merchants went belly up. We didn't get any notice and no severance pay. They just put the firing slip in our time clock slot."

"How long have you been there? Didn't you get that job right after high school?"

"Well, almost. I had that burger job for almost two years. Then, I was off for almost a year before getting this job at Merchants. I've got almost ten years there now, but that is all down the drain."

"Got anything lined up?"

"No, we just got the news today. I was wondering if you still have that old RV trailer."

"Yeah. It's over at Tobin's rental house. I can't park it here."

"Who is Tobin?"

"He's a cop and has a big house and few rentals around town."

"So, perhaps I could borrow the RV for a while?"

TROUBLE WITH ALICE

"Sure. Where do you want it?"

"I'll have to check on that and get back to you. You're a life saver, Carl."

W̲here would I be without this truck and trailer from Carl? Homeless, that's what. He's a true friend. Tobin's renter was happy to get it off the property, too. He didn't say so, but I could tell he was happy to get rid of it. Well, here's the park and my space, number twenty-two. Nice tree for some shade.

Alice pulls the trailer into the space and gets out of the truck. She attaches the sewer, water, and electric plug-in before pulling down the stabling jacks. Once done, she unhooks the trailer from the truck and eyeballs it for level.

She notices a woman in the next space watching her every move. Alice decides to pretend there is a man inside.

Heading for an open window, she yells, "Is it level, Lester?" She pauses, pretending he is talking to her. "Okay, I'm going to set the jacks."

That was easy. Now to see if it really is level.

She steps into the trailer and grabs a small bowl from the cupboard. Alice fills it halfway with water and sets it on the table.

That's not too bad, just a little lean to the left. I'll live with it. Now back to the apartment to get the rest of my things. I don't know what I'll do with that big queen-sized bed. I'll ask the super to buy it.

Back at the apartment complex, she takes the elevator to the third floor. The small hallway leads to the super's apartment. He likes the view from the higher apartment and the fact that no one is making noise or walking around above him. He has the entire third floor to himself.

Alice wonders if he ever has guests. She knows he has a young boy that does all of his grocery shopping. She notices the faded wall-to-wall green carpet. The walls are a pale blue. Two small lights sit on either side of a skylight in the ceiling. Everything is dirty, as if nothing has been cleaned in years. Unable to find a button to ring a bell, she knocks on the door.

"Who's there?" a voice hollers from behind the door.

"It's me, Alice Grey."

"I thought you moved out. You left a pile of junk up there."

"That wasn't junk. I piled those boxes in the center of the room so I could come back and get them."

TROUBLE WITH ALICE

"I've already rented the place to someone else."

"Open the door so we can talk without yelling."

Irritated, Alice knocks hard on the door.

The sound of shuffling feet echoes in the distance. Locks click. The door swings open several inches.

"Okay. What do you want?" the super mumbles without opening the door any further.

He keeps his face hidden. The strong scent of smoke surrounds him and escapes into the hall.

Alice steps back a few feet and covers her nose with one hand.

"I was wondering if you or someone in the building would like to buy my queen-sized bed."

"I already gave that to eighteen."

"But it's mine!" Alice cries. "You can't give it away until my lease runs out and that's not until Saturday."

"Well, I did. You should have told me you would be back. I'm busy." The super reaches for the door's handle, intent on closing it. "Go see eighteen if you think you still want it."

"Is the rest of my stuff still up there?" Alice yells, holding a foot out to keep the door from closing.

The foul odor causes her to gag. She presses her hand to her nose once more and turns her head to one side.

"I don't know. I called the Salvation Army. They said they would be here today."

"I'll sue you if those boxes have been touched. I

have until Saturday to move out."

"Remove your foot."

Alice growls and steps aside.

The door swings shut with an audible thud.

She heads back to her apartment, wanting to make sure that all of her belongings are there. A sigh of relief escapes her upon seeing the boxes stacked in the center of the room.

"The boxes haven't been moved. That's a good thing. I wouldn't have anything to wear. I better go to eighteen and see what I can do about the bed. But first, I better load up the truck."

Alice grabs several of the boxes and takes them to the pick-up. It isn't long before she's done. She re-enters the apartment complex and approaches the direction board in the lobby. She points to eighteen.

"There it is on the second floor."

She heads for the elevator, hitting the button and waiting for it to arrive. Once the doors open, she steps inside. The strong smell of cigarettes causes her to gag again. She pushes a button and rides the cab to the second floor.

Apartment eighteen faces the elevator door. This floor doesn't have wall-to-wall carpeting. The well-worn tile hasn't been cleaned in a very long time. A single light bulb dangles from the ceiling at each end of the long hallway. Light trickles in through dirty windows.

Alice approaches the door to the apartment, knocking gently upon a panel that appears to be cleaner than the area around the handle.

"Who is it?" a woman asks, a minute later.

"Alice Grey from four."

"What do you want?"

"I want to talk to you about the queen-sized bed the super gave you. Open the door and we won't have to shout."

"Go away. I paid the super three hundred dollars for this bed. What do you want with it?"

"You paid the super three hundred dollars for my bed? He said he gave it to you. It's my bed. The super stole it from me. Open the door."

"Well, go talk to him. It's my bed now."

"I'm calling the cops. You've got stolen property. That's a crime, you know."

"If you don't go away, I'll call the cops."

Alice doesn't have a cellphone, so she must to go back to her apartment to call the police. She dials the number and asks for Officer Tobin or Detective Harris. Both are unavailable.

"I need to speak to anyone that would handle the theft of my bed."

"I don't understand your problem, ma'am. Can you explain it to me?"

"The super in my apartment building stole my queen-sized bed, all the sheets and pillows, and then sold it to the tenant in apartment eighteen. She said she paid the super three hundred dollars for it. Did I speak slowly enough? By the way, what is your name?"

"I'm Officer Frank. Do you have any more information to substantiate your claim?"

"What more do you want? Send someone over here to get my bed back."

"I'll turn this over to burglary. They should contact you in three or four days."

"Hey, Frank. I need someone here today. Now! I need my bed."

"I don't know what their caseload is so I can't tell you when someone will contact you."

"Okay, here's what I'm going to do. I'm taking my little hammer up to number eighteen. She will get mad and call you guys. I'll be there pounding on her door when someone gets here for this domestic disturbance and con-game. And they can get my bed for me."

Two officers answer number eighteen's call about Alice's pounding on her door. They arrive just in time to see the super grabbing her and knocking her down.

An officer immediately seizes the super.

The other officer approaches Alice, gently pulling her into a sitting position.

"Are you hurt, ma'am?" Tobin asks, placing his hand on her shoulder.

TROUBLE WITH ALICE

"Did you see that? Did you see that crook hit me? He's the one that broke into my apartment and stole my bed. Then, he sold it to this woman in eighteen."

Tobin notices the bruise on the side of Alice's jaw. He assumes the super caused it and calls out to the other officer.

"Jerry, we'll have to call for a medic. This poor woman has a large bruise developing on her face." He turns back to her. "I'll see if we can get the occupants of this apartment to open up and get some ice for you. You stay there and stay calm. Hey, didn't I meet you at the bank robbery last week?"

"I don't know. There was so much going on, I didn't take time to remember every face."

"I'll take this one down to the car and be right back. Okay, no more hitting ladies for you, Mister. Let's go," Officer Jerry says, snapping a pair of handcuffs around the super's wrists before shoving him along the hallway.

Alice smiles.

The super protests, "She was the one banging on the apartment door."

Jerry ignores him.

They disappear down the stairs.

"So, are we going to get my bed out of this apartment now, Officer Tobin?" she coos.

"I'll see if they will answer." He knocks on the door. "Police, open the door, please. Police."

"Go away. I won't be tricked by that. Go away

before I call the cops," the woman says, unwilling to open the door.

"I *am* the police. I'm Officer Tobin. Open the door, please, and you will see my uniform and badge."

"I've got a dog in here. Don't try anything funny."

"Please, open the door. I'll stand back a ways so you can see me."

"Don't you try any tricks!" The door opens slightly. The lady glances at Officer Tobin. "Where's the super? I gotta see someone I know."

"We had to take him down to the station for assault. Can you see me now?"

The woman frowns. Her mouth thins to a tight line.

"You look awful young to be a cop."

"Yes, ma'am. A lot of people say that. Now, may we come in?"

He reaches out and gently pushes on the door.

The woman sighs and steps aside. "Who is that on the floor? Did you hit her?"

She struggles to close the door.

Tobin is stronger and pushes it open, pausing in the doorway. "Just look at me, ma'am. I'm a policeman in full uniform and this is my badge. If you like, get a pencil and paper to write the number down. I won't move."

"I don't need a pencil and paper. Who do you think I am? A dummy?"

"Ask her about my bed," Alice yells, standing up

TROUBLE WITH ALICE

and walking into the apartment. "She's got my bed."

"She's a liar. I paid three hundred dollars for it."

"There's your proof, Officer. The super stole my bed and sold it to this woman. It's stolen property, and I want it back right now. And also all those sheets and pillows that go with it."

"I'm going to have it impounded and get this all sorted out by the judge."

The corners of Alice's mouth tilt downward. "So what do I sleep on?"

A lice mutters to herself all the way back to the trailer park and her camper.

"Damn, people. Steal my bed, and now that cop says he has to get a judge to see who is lying. I won't get my bed back for a month of Sundays. I won't want it by then with all the cigarette odor embedded in it."

She pulls into her space. On the way home, she'd bought several items of men's clothing, intending to hang them on the line outside to make people think a man is waiting for her inside the trailer.

"I'm home, honey," she yells, unlocking the door and entering the RV. "I suppose I'll have to sleep on these seat cushions. There's no room in here for that bed anyway. In fact, I guess the impound is a good place to store it until I get another job and a new place to stay. Hell, it's even got police protection twenty-four-seven."

She spends the rest of the afternoon bringing in the boxes from her apartment. Alice spots a woman in a space across the driveway watching her. She decides to continue her ruse. She opens the door and throws a pair of men's work boots out on the ground.

"How many times do I have to tell you, Lester?" she yells. "No dirty work boots in the house!"

Alice slams the door shut and sinks to the floor, laughing quietly.

That ought to get the spy thinking.

CHAPTER SIX

THE COURTSHIP

Alice spends the next several days looking for work without results. She is ready to take any job in order to get a paycheck.

Sitting at the table, she counts her remaining cash.

"No lobster and prime rib for you, gal. It's going to be two meals a day with a choice of two hot dogs, or macaroni and cheese for the duration. You've got to save money for bus fare and gas. I'll give the unemployment office my new address tomorrow, and maybe I can get my first check. I wonder how much that will be. Bedtime, Alice. Another day tomorrow."

The sun wakes her long before the alarm goes off.

"I should have closed the blinds. Man, that sun is bright today. Well, Alice, what's for breakfast? Hot dogs, or mac and cheese? Why did I forget to buy buns for this dog? I guess a slice of bread will do, and then I'll go to the unemployment office."

"This isn't so bad. Two hundred and eight a week. Off to the bank, Alice. We need cash to buy food."

Food Store is a few blocks from the unemployment office. She finds a parking space at the far end of the lot. She considers it part of her walking requirement to stay fit. A branch office of her bank is located within the store, allowing her to cash the check. Alice strolls down the produce aisle, spotting a familiar face.

Is that Officer Tobin?

She approaches from the rear, gently bumping his cart. "Oops, sorry."

Tobin turns in her direction. "No harm. Was I in the way?" He recognizes Alice. "Hey, do I know you? The lady from the bank and the stolen bed, right?"

Alice smiles and nods, too embarrassed because of her actions. "That's me, the lady with the stolen bed. What a way to be known."

"You look nice today. I notice the bruise on your cheek is almost gone. Does it still hurt?"

"Nah, it's okay. So, you do the shopping instead of your wife?"

"I'm not married. I shop for myself."

She scans his cart and notes the wine and steaks. "Big party tonight?"

"Why do you say that?"

"Just noticing you have four bottles of wine, some steaks, and is that brie cheese on top of the crackers?"

"I guess you might think that." Tobin laughs. "But I like this wine, and what else besides cheese and crackers, do you have with a nice glass of wine? So, what kind of wine do you have with your husband?"

Alice laughs. "No husband. Not even a boyfriend. Just me. I think we have that issue settled." She pauses. "Don't look at my cart like that. I had to move and restock the fridge."

She turns her cart away.

"I wonder what you would say if I were to ask you to share my cheese and wine this evening."

"Well, I don't know." Alice smiles. She tilts her head to the side and raises an eyebrow. "Why don't you ask and find out, Officer Tobin?"

"If I did ask you to share some wine and cheese, you would have to drop the officer part and just call me Tobin."

Alice curls a hand around her chin, while staring

at the ceiling and pretending to think. "Hmm, Tobin, eh?"

"That's only if I did ask you, and you did accept."

"For gosh sakes," a lady standing nearby butts in. "Quit the garbage talk and ask her, Mr. Tobin. And you, young lady, if you don't answer soon, I'll take him. Quit the shenanigans and say yes. What are you two waiting for? A chaperone, or a bang on your noggins?"

Tobin and Alice laugh, reaching for each other's hands.

"If you ask, Mr. Tobin, I will accept."

"Will you join me for an evening of wine tasting with a few crackers and cheese?"

"I would be delighted. Where and what time?"

"I'll write the address down for you." Tobin pulls a small notebook and pen from one of his pockets. He jots down the information, rips off the page, and hands it to her. "Here you are, Alice. See you at seven-thirty."

She accepts the slip of paper.

"Well, thank the gods in heaven, that's settled. I can finish my shopping in peace," the lady says, pushing her cart away.

TROUBLE WITH ALICE

Alice arrives at her camper and notices the nosy neighbor watching.
Time for some more of Lester.

She opens the door and steps inside. "Damn it, Lester. What is that smell? Did you burn something on the range again?"

Alice slams the door shut.

That ought to keep her for a while.

By the time she stows her groceries and takes a shower, it is almost seven. What to wear is the next question.

Well, only four choices in your wardrobe. Close your eyes and pick one.

I don't think the red one is right for a first date. Crap, put it on anyway. It's the best you've got.

Tobin's home is easy to find. Alice parks her truck beside what she assumes is his car.

"Wow, a new Caddy. Not bad for a cop's salary. And this house must be worth a pretty penny."

"Come in, Alice," Tobin says, opening the door, seconds later. "Everything is waiting for you. Wine is chilled. Crackers and cheese are ready. All we need is you. Come in, please."

He's wearing a soft camel dinner jacket over a white shirt with pale sandy-colored slacks and tan slippers. The foyer opens into a large room with a wide, curved staircase leading to the second story. Large paintings of men and women line the wall on the left side. The carpet is a plush light blue with oriental throw rugs at the entrance of each room.

Alice glances about the room. Three chandeliers hang from the high ceiling, but only the wall sconces are on.

Tobin offers her his arm. "May I escort the lady to the drawing room? My mother always called it that. I just call it the lounge. I hang out here most of time when I'm home."

She wraps a hand around his arm.

They walk to an open arch on the right side of the large entryway.

"I had the doors removed here because I'm alone and they were open all the time anyway."

Alice pauses inside the room. A large television screen stands to the left with three lounge chairs arranged in front of it a few feet away. To the right stands a desk with what looks like an old-fashioned lamp with a green shade, several papers, and a photo frame on it without a picture.

That's strange. No photo.

The back of an office chair peeks from behind.

"I had the cleaning gal fix things up a bit for you. Usually, this room gets a bit messy. I've got the wine and some other stuff straight ahead in what I call my reading area."

Several large paintings of men and women adorn

the back wall. She catches sight of a wet bar with refrigerated wine storage below. A cherry wood table sits in front of it with eight cushioned chairs.

"I put everything on the cart, so we could sit here or by the television. Maybe a movie or . . . just talk. Whatever we . . ."

Her silence makes him nervous.

"So, what is your pleasure, ma'am?"

"Let's try the bar area for a while. I must admit I'm a little speechless right now."

She sits down and folds her arms across her lap.

"I remodeled this so-called parlor because I thought it should be used for more than just weddings and funerals. Mother, of course, objected some, but she agreed when I had the interior designer show her the color plans for the room."

"Is your mother up there on the wall?"

"That's her in the middle." He points to the picture. "It was painted when she was about eighty, as I recall. Dad is on her left, and my brother and sister are at each end."

"Where are you?"

"I haven't got around to it yet. Somehow, I'm not interested. Who's to see it now that I am the last of the family?"

"What about your brother and sister?"

"Auto accident. Both died. But let's get on with the wine tasting. I thought a pale red for the crackers to start."

Tobin grabs two glasses from the cart. He

uncorks the bottle and pours a small amount into one of the glasses. He raises it to his nose, swirling the wine gently before taking a sip.

"Not bad for only ten years old." He pours a bit of wine into another glass and offers it to Alice. "Here you go. What do you think?"

"Do I swirl, smell, and sip, too?"

"Of course, why not? Tell me what you think."

"I haven't done this before. I just open the flap on the boxed wine and go to it."

"I think you have a point there. Drink the damn stuff. To hell with the snobs."

He pours more of the wine into their glasses. He sets the glass down and motions to Alice to drink.

"I have to drive home and can't drink too much on an empty stomach. I might get drunk and get stopped for DUI. You get stopped on the way to bail me out, and you join me in the holding tank."

He laughs. "How about a few crackers? I've got four or five different cheeses there to choose from. Take your pick. Later, a surprise."

"Time for the big event. Come with me." Tobin offers her his arm. "We are off to the surprise."

Alice is somewhat reluctant, but his charm wears

TROUBLE WITH ALICE

her down. She takes his arm.

He leads her back to the large foyer, taking a right turn toward a double door. As they approach, the doors open.

Two ladies wearing aprons smile at Alice and usher them inside. The room has a long dining table with a white tablecloth and a lace border. Four silver vases are filled with red roses. Three additional vases have gardenias in full white bloom. Faint fragrances from all the flowers fill the air. Settings for two have been placed at the far end of the table.

Tobin leads her to one of the chairs, pulling it out for her.

She opens her mouth to speak.

He places a gentle finger to her lips. Once he's satisfied that she's settled into her chair, he sits down adjacent to her.

Alice opens her mouth once more, but only gets one word out. "Tobin . . ."

He holds a finger to his lips and smiles. He reaches for a bottle of wine chilling in a bucket of ice, uncorks it, and pours a small amount into two glasses.

The women enter the room, placing a salad dish and a revolving stand with several dressings in small cups on it. The stand is placed between them and their plates are placed in front of them. Without a sound, they smile and leave.

"I took the liberty of watching what you put in your cart at Food Store, so this should match your greenery choices."

Alice smiles, relieved that the surprise is an intimate dinner for two. "Do I dare ask what the rest of this divine surprise entails?"

"Wouldn't it be better if the surprise continues? We have the rest of the evening, don't we?"

"I guess so. I don't have to work tomorrow."

"I asked the ladies to choose the appetizer, but I think they may have gone overboard with it. I do hope you eat crab stuffed in mushrooms. You're not allergic to them, are you?"

"I don't think so. I usually eat about anything, but of course, it's a lot of the fast food stuff. There are no stuffed mushrooms at King's Pizza that I know of."

"Let's serve you some now then. But first, a small swig of wine to cleanse the pallet."

Tobin waves his hand.

One of the ladies appears. Her hands are wrapped around a plate with four stuffed mushrooms on it. She places it on the table and walks away.

"Some people eat these with a fork and knife, but I prefer my fingers." Tobin reaches for a mushroom. "Go ahead. Try one."

Alice picks up one of the mushrooms and takes a small nibble. She chews quietly and nods.

"Not too bad, Mr. Tobin. Not too bad."

She takes a larger bite.

They exchange smiles and sly glances.

I'm beginning to like this guy. Enough that he is obviously rich and a looker. I doubt I can fit here. I didn't even know what crab stuffed mushrooms were.

She glances at Tobin again.

He reaches for another mushroom and smiles.

I guess he is waiting for me to say something. What?

She swallows the last bite and reaches for her glass.

"Oh, do you need a refill?"

"This is fine. What did you say? I need to cleanse my pallet. I think I have enough wine for one evening. Remember, I have to drive home."

"Are you ready for the entrée?"

"I'm not sure."

"You'll love it." He raises a hand a few inches in the air and smiles once more. "In a minute, you will have the best steak you have ever tasted."

"Do you realize how long we have been drinking?"

"My Russian friends would say, 'As long as you eat while drinking, you will be okay.'"

"I don't know any Russians. Do you travel a lot?"

"Not so much anymore. Oh, here comes the chef with our steaks. Dig in and let me know how you like it."

The chef arrives, wearing a white coat and toque, placing a covered silver dish in front of her, gently lifting the lid to reveal the steak still sizzling on a black cast-iron plate with a wooden plate underneath.

Alice pulls back.

Tobin notices her reaction. "I like the cast-iron

plate to help keep the food hot. Someday, I'm going to install those induction hot plates on the table."

"Induction hot plates? What's that?"

"It's a magnetic gadget that keeps the iron plate hot. Perfectly safe. You can place your hand on the so-called burner area and not get burned. They turn off in about thirty seconds if they don't have a plate on it. A whole bunch of other safeties, too."

"Expensive, I bet."

"Not really, but let's eat. We can talk science later."

Alice nods and takes a small bite. She smiles and notes the very faint pink in the center and grill marks on both sides.

Something tells me I'm eating a very expensive chunk of beef. So tender.

Tobin interrupts her thoughts. "So, how is it?"

"Like I'm in heaven. Do you always eat and drink like this?"

"Nah." He laughs. "Mostly, I eat peanut butter and jelly sandwiches with a side dish of yogurt."

"And lots of coffee?"

"I gave up coffee years ago. People started asking me if I took a cup to bed with me. I figured I must be drinking too much and quit."

"Cold turkey?" Alice asks between swallows.

"Yep. No more coffee."

"So you just drink wine now?"

"Mostly a lot of water with a dash of Coke for color and a bit of taste."

TROUBLE WITH ALICE

Alice enjoys the steak and consumes it all, wiping her lips several times with the napkin on her lap, being careful not to stain the embroidery.

"I think it's time for me to go home."

"I hope you will come again. Maybe tomorrow evening?"

"We shall see. I need to find a job."

"I might be able to help with that. What do you do?"

"I barely made it through high school. After a short time at Freddie's Fast Food, I got the job at Merchants in an area near their assembly line. I had to check all the invoices, but that's gone now. They went bankrupt, and we all lost our jobs."

"Don't you worry. I've got a friend who will find skills you don't even know you have. Give me your cell number, and I'll have her call you."

"Don't have one."

"No cellphone?"

"Nope."

"Number at home?"

"Nope."

"I can fix that. There's an extra cellphone in my desk. You can have it."

"Why are you doing all this?"

Tobin sits back in his chair. His eyes bore deep into hers. Silence descends upon them. Several minutes pass before he leans forward, pressing his elbows against the edge of the table.

With enthusiasm, he says, "Alice, let's call Cassy

right now. I usually call her about now every night anyway. You talk to her and make a date to meet somewhere for lunch or afternoon tea. At the library, for gosh sakes. Anywhere. Just meet her."

He doesn't move, waiting for her to answer.

Confusion races through her mind.

What is this? Who is Cassy? He hasn't made any rude advances to you. Well, Alice, make up your mind.

Finally, she nods and says, "Okay."

"Just a minute. Don't move. I'll get my phone and bring it in here on speaker so you can hear everything."

He stands and dashes out of the room, returning in minutes. Tobin sets a cellphone down in front of Alice and places another on the table between them. He dials Cassy's number and turns on the speakerphone.

His friend soon answers the call. "Hello, Tobin. What's new tonight?"

"I have someone here I want you to meet."

"Okay. Who, what, when, where, and why?"

Tobin glances at Alice. "Cassy was an editor for a few years and always uses the five doubles."

"Did you say a few years? More like sixty, and I'm still doing it. Where is the lady?"

"How did you know it was a lady?"

"If it was a man, you would have taken care of whatever this is by yourself."

"Cassy, I want you to meet my guest, Alice. She is sitting right here at the table. Say hello."

"Hello."

"Talk to her, Alice. Make a date."

"Is that your name? Alice?"

"Yes, ma'am."

"If you ever call me ma'am again, I'll spank your hide. Call me Cassy. Now tell me, what is going on over there?"

"I want you two to meet and talk about skills Alice may have. She needs a job because her last place went bankrupt."

"I can do that. Are you listening, Alice?"

"Yes, ma—ah, Cassy."

"Where do you live?"

"Right now at the trailer park on Davidson Street until I find another job and get another apartment."

"Do you know that little coffee shop on Third Street near the post office?"

"Yes. It's near my old place."

"Can you meet me there tomorrow around one?"

"Yes. I think so."

"Don't *think* so. Yes, or no? I want you to start thinking positive. No more thinks, got it?"

"Yes, I can meet you. How will I know who you are?"

"I'll be the lady with the green feather in her bonnet."

"Thank you, Cassy," Tobin says, disconnecting the phone call.

"So, who is that?"

"A very dear friend I've known all my life. You'll

love her. How about dessert?"

"I'm stuffed, and it's past my bedtime. I better go."

CHAPTER SEVEN

MEETING CASSY

A lice enters the coffee shop. A counter in front of the back wall stands directly in front of her with backless round red-covered stools. The American flag hangs high on the wall. A coffee station with stacked mugs on each side takes up most of the lower part of the wall. Photos of what must be local heroes adorn the rest of the shop's walls. Almost all of the tables are occupied with lunch patrons.

A waitress passes in front of her. She smiles.

"Good afternoon, Miss. Take any table. I'll be right back with a menu."

Two men at a nearby table look up and smile.

Alice scans the tables and spots Cassy, who's sitting by a window.

There's the lady with the green feather. She looks like . . .

I don't know . . . fabulous. She must be in her seventies. I hope I look that good at her age. Well, here goes nothing.

The lady waves at her. "Hello, Alice. Come and sit with me. We have a lot to talk about. What do you drink?"

I wonder how she knew me. They must have talked about me after I left last night. I guess I don't have anything to lose.

"I'll order a plain coffee and come back."

"Nonsense. Sit down. I can handle this."

Alice approaches and takes the nearest chair.

Cassy waves a hand in the air.

A waitress approaches the table.

"Plain coffee for my guest. Cream and sugar?"

"No thank you. Black is fine."

The waitress nods and jots down her order. She turns and walks away, heading for the kitchen.

"So . . . What can I do for you, young lady?"

"I thought Tobin would have briefed you all about me."

"Nope. Never said a word. He's like that. You'll have to tell me."

"He thinks you might be able to discover some sort of hidden talent I have for a new job."

"What talents do you have?"

"I'm not sure I have any special talents, unless you count working at that burger place. Later, I did most of the paperwork keeping track of the stock and invoices at Merchants."

"I don't want you going back to that burger joint and clerking will never pay much." She rubs her chin and stares at Alice. "A job hunt is sometimes a very difficult problem to solve. Let me ask you a question. Have you ever sat down and tried to write about the things you can do?"

"No. I can't say I have."

"Good. Let's do it now." She rummages through her purse and withdraws a small notepad, ready to ask questions and write them down. "Any brothers or sisters?"

"No. Family all gone. I'm alone."

"Did you ever do any babysitting growing up?"

"Nope."

"What was your first job?" She catches sight of the waitress. "Oh, here comes Sara with your coffee and a menu."

Sara weaves in and out through the randomly placed tables, nodding at several diners and saying good morning to others. She stops and addresses someone before heading in Cassy and Alice's direction. With a flick of her hand, she sets a mug and menu on the table.

"Just raise your hand. One of us will take your order," she says, and leaves.

Alice nods and takes a sip of the coffee. She sets the mug down.

"Boy, that is much too hot to drink. I worked at a fast food restaurant for two years. Then, I worked at a desk near the assembly line, checking invoices at Merchants for almost ten years."

"I heard that name. What do they make?"

"Mostly a line of baby cribs. If I finished the invoices, I was supposed to put the rattle on the top rail as the crib passed by me to relieve the task of a person down the line who was doing three different things."

"That's all you did for eight hours a day?"

"We had a ten-minute break in the morning and afternoon, and half an hour for lunch."

"You drive a car, right?"

"Yes."

"Stick shift or automatic?"

"I can do both. I'm using a friend's pick-up truck right now. It's a stick shift."

"Tobin didn't make this very easy. How about hobbies? Do you sew, knit, or throw darts in the pub? Anything?"

"I guess not. I'm usually pretty tired by the time I get home every night. Weekends, I get groceries, do the laundry, or whatever other errands are necessary."

"You need a husband and about ten kids to take care of. That would get your blood moving."

"I guess a husband might be okay, but I don't know about ten kids." Alice snickers. "I live in a borrowed camper right now. There's hardly enough room for me, and I don't know what I'll do if I get my bed back from the impound."

"Whoa, stop right there. Your bed is in the impound with the police?"

"It's a bit complicated. The bottom line is, the super where I used to live sold my bed to one of the tenants. Now there is all sorts of red tape in getting it back."

"What does the unemployment office say? Are they giving you any places to apply for work?"

"No, I just tell them where I've made applications, and they give me two hundred and eight dollars a week. That's enough for bus fare around town, groceries, and some fast food stuff for lunch."

"Okay, where have you made applications?"

"I try to go to places within walking distance from the bus stops. They all want a telephone number, but I don't have one. Then, they ask for a cellphone number. I didn't have one of those either, so Tobin gave me a cell he wasn't using. Most places, of course, want a work history. The ones that read it in front of me shake their heads and say, 'Sorry.' When I try to go back, the front desk turns me down before I can even talk to the boss."

"Do you like animals? Cats and dogs, for example?"

"I've never had a pet, but I guess I don't mind them."

"Here's what we're going to do. I'm taking you down to my vet's office and getting you a job today. It may be messy. He may just have clean-up duties for you, but it'll give you some experience to put on your applications, and I'll see that he pays more than the unemployment. Who knows? You may even like it. Come on. Let's go right now."

Two hours later, Alice says goodbye to Cassy.

That was easy. You've got a job and start tomorrow at three-fifty a week working part-time so I can look for something better.

CHAPTER EIGHT

HAPPY DAYS AHEAD

Tobin and Alice are having lunch at a small cafe on Third Street.

It's a run-of-the-mill place. Framed farm scenes hang on red-colored walls. Wooden tables have several initials carved into their worn surfaces. Several chairs wobble. The location's saving grace is the fact that the food is great.

A waitress and a young man wait nearby. Both are cheerful, neatly dressed, and groomed.

"How are things at the kennel?" Tobin asks, looking over the menu.

"I can't thank you and Cassy enough. I need to find a new place to live, though. That trailer park is okay, except for the nosy woman next door. Remember, I told you about her calling the cops?"

"No, you didn't."

"Seems like my scheme to make everyone think I had a man inside backfired. One of them called the cops because they'd seen me chopping something up in the bed of the truck. Later, they snuck over and caught sight of a lot of blood scattered across the vehicle's bed. They called the cops and said I killed Lester."

"Who's Lester?"

"The imaginary man."

"Then what happened?"

"The cops arrested me. I spent two days in jail while their lab tested the blood and found it wasn't human. It was fish, like I tried to tell them a hundred times. They even searched inside the RV."

"Why didn't you call me?"

"This happened long before we started dating on a regular basis. I'm tired of the stares, closing doors, and seeing shades pulled down on windows at the park."

"That's all in the past. Forget about them. You can have the east wing and move in with me."

Tobin's suggestion stuns Alice.

I guess it has come to this. Living at his house? Not sure about that.

"So what do you say, Alice? It's got a separate entrance. You could come and go whenever you like. I can get the carpenters to close it off from the rest of the building. It would be like renting an apartment or a condo, only free. Not only that, but I might be able to get your bed out of impound."

TROUBLE WITH ALICE

Should I or not? That is the question.

We see each other every day for lunch or dinner, depending on his shift. He's a cop. It should be safe. I still can't get over that. I'm dating a handsome cop, and he says I might get my bed back. That would be nice to get off the cushions in the camper.

"You can move in on Saturday. I can get a few guys to help, and the carpenters can come on Monday."

I guess we're growing closer to each other. Not only meals, but he takes me to concerts and the movies. We shop together at Food Store and see that woman once in a while. She is one sweet lady.

Never overnight with Tobin, but every day, a gentle hug when we meet, and one when we part. Would he expect more with me living there?

I wonder what it would be like to kiss him. We have been seeing each other for over three months already. Would I expect more? Would he expect more? That's the question. Although he did say he would close off the wing.

"What do you say? This Saturday, or the next?"

"What did you say about Saturday?"

"Move into the east wing."

"I work this Saturday, but I guess the following one would be okay."

It would be the end of the month, and the rent is due. Find a place for the camper. Sleep in my own queen-sized bed again. Can't do that, though. It's still at the impound. I could buy a bedroll and sleep on the floor. Did I just tell him okay?

"More coffee, anyone?" the waitress asks,

breaking through her daydream.

"Alice?"

Still thinking about the move, she doesn't answer.

Tobin waves the waitress away.

The intercom rings in the east wing.

"Good morning, Tobin. What's up?"

"I thought we would go shopping this morning. Can I come over?"

"Give me about ten minutes."

"May I come in a moment?" Tobin asks.

"Door is open. Come on in," Alice yells from her bedroom.

He enters the room and stands near a table with fresh flowers on it.

"Good morning," she says, turning around and hugging him.

Tobin kneels.

Her eyes open wide. Alice's heart hammers deep within her chest.

Is this going to be a proposal?

"I love you, Alice, and want to marry you. Will you say yes?"

He's asking me to marry him, and we haven't even kissed yet. What if that doesn't go well, and I have already said yes?

"I'll need a hug and kiss first."

He stands. With a gentle, but firm embrace, he kisses her.

Both are reluctant to end it.

She draws back and stares into his eyes.

How can I be so lucky? If he is as good in bed as this, I'll be happy forever.

Holding him close, she says, "Yes, Tobin. I'll marry you. But do I still sleep in the east wing?"

"Not if I have anything to say about it. Let's go shopping for a ring."

Connect with Donald Kemp online via the following social media outlets to keep up-to-date on what's coming next for him and his books.

WEBSITE:

https://donkempauthor.com

FACEBOOK:

https://www.facebook.com/DonaldKempAuthor

TWITTER:

http://www.twitter.com/DonKempAuthor

GOODREADS:

https://www.goodreads.com/author/show/14933726.Donald_Kemp

EMAIL:

don.kemp.author@gmail.com

Please enjoy this short story, a collaboration written by Donald Kemp and John Bauer, winner of The Gray Tree Collaboration Contest.

DONALD KEMP
CONTRIBUTING AUTHOR,
JOHN BAUER

THE GRAY TREE

COLD, HUNGRY, AND LOST, I paused beside a large tree. I hoped to hear Mother's dinner bell ringing in the distance. Instead, I heard an unexpected voice speaking to me.

"You're standing on my feet."

I turned around and slowly walked around the tree in search of the voice's origin. "I must be hearing things. There's no one here."

"You are still standing on my feet," the irate voice replied.

I looked down, raising one foot, and then the other. The ground beneath my feet was covered with the tree's fallen leaves.

Nothing.

An annoyed sigh sounded nearby. "If you don't mind, I would appreciate it if you would please step back a little."

The cold must be getting to my brain. I'm hearing things.

I took a step back from the tree and waited.

"Aah. Thank you," the voice said.

A slight frown marred my forehead. Where is the voice coming from? There's nothing here but a simple tree.

"Now this is getting ridiculous. Trees don't talk."

"Who told you that?" the tree asked. "I'm a tree, and I can talk. I also have feet. Don't you have feet?"

I glanced down at my bare toes. "Yes, of course, I do have feet."

The tree chuckled. "You silly humans call my feet, roots."

"Well, I suppose that's what they are—roots."

"And just what do your feet do?"

I never thought about trying to analyze the purpose of my feet. The appendages were just an extension of my body that helped me to move around. I looked down in contemplation.

"I guess they hold me up."

"That's what my feet do, too. They hold me up."

"Speaking of feet, do you happen to know where I could warm my feet? They're freezing."

"Of course, they're freezing. You ran out into the cold without any shoes or socks. Why not find a nice spot and dig a hole? Then slide your feet inside the hole and cover them up with dirt like mine. And while we're at it, why did you wake me up? I just finished taking off my red fall dress. Imagine my surprise to

THE GRAY TREE

find that someone stepped on my feet and woke me up," the tree said, and sighed dramatically. "By the way, you're stepping on my very nice red dress."

I looked down to find that I now stood within a small pile of leaves.

"Enough. No more talk about feet. Are you a witch of some sort? I'm Jerry, by the way. As to your nice red dress, you threw it on the ground for anyone to walk on. Could you do me a favor, though? Can you tell me which way is north so I can find my way back home?"

The tree chortled once more. Several branches crackled overhead.

"That's easy. Just look for some moss. They say it always grows on the north side of trees. Now, I'm going back to sleep."

I took a moment to examine the tree. Its bark was bare. Not a speck of moss lay in sight.

"Wait!" I cried, my voice full of panic. "You are the only tree in sight, and there is no sign of moss on you."

"Moss? I'm not a vegan. What would I do with moss?"

"I don't suppose you could use one of your limbs and point me in the right direction? You seem to know everything else."

"See, you did it again. My limbs, as you called them, happen to be my beautiful, long, and slender arms. And if I had a mind to help you, I suppose I could point the way."

I looked up as the tree shuddered in the wind.

"It's that way," the tree said before drifting off to sleep.

The slight wind pushed its limbs in every direction, making it hard for me to discern the direction in which it pointed.

A sigh of frustration burst from my lips. If they were arms and not limbs, why couldn't he—or she, for who can tell the difference—point one of them properly to guide my way?

Feet . . . For gosh sakes, whoever heard of trees having feet? If they had feet, they could go anywhere they wanted.

A vivid image rose to the surface of my mind. I saw Mother standing near the grove, her brow furrowed. Her dainty hands were curled into fists and pressed against her hips.

"I wonder what happened to our apple tree."

"He went south for the winter," the peach tree replied.

"No, you're thinking of the banana tree," Mother replied. "She must have tropical weather if she's to produce fruit."

The peach tree shook a random branch. "She eloped with the coconut tree. No bowling tourneys any longer."

A smile spread across Mother's lips. "They'll return. When spring rolls around again, of course."

"And the apple tree? What became of him?"

"He followed a John Chapman fellow 'cause he was so kindly disposed to apples. Said he was a crusading apple farmer spreading seed all over the Midwest. Guess I answered my own question."

THE GRAY TREE

"That leaves me, the oak, the walnut, and the Scottish Pine," the peach tree said.

My imagination grabbed me, like the gray tree's roots clutched the earth. I further envisioned the conversation taking place between Mother and the tree.

Mother sighed and shook her head. "You'll be heading back to Georgia soon. Back to your roots, so to speak. You've got family there."

"You've been good to me, Mother, in taking all my fruit and never letting one go to waste."

She approached the tree and pressed a hand against its gnarled bark. Mother patted it, the same way she would pat me on the head when I would do something wrong as a child. Tilting her head, she stared at the tree's leaves rustling with sorrow above her.

"Could only eat and give away so many peaches. Canned the rest. Going to miss you something fierce. Hope some of your kin come north to spend my final years with me."

A lone branch descended. Its leafed tip curled around Mother's shoulders.

"Going to miss you, too, Mother. I'll tell my cousins about you and send some your way."

Mother rubbed her hand across the bark. A bright sheen of moisture shone in her eyes.

"Unfortunately, the oak is old and stubborn, and the walnut has gone wild over the cherry. I've decided both must be put down. I'm going to bring them inside. Make them into a table and chairs, and a bedroom suite. Don't tell them. They'll be with me for the rest of my life."

The peach tree chuckled. "And the Scottish Pine?"

"Silly, you know I dig him up every Christmas and replant him after New Year's. I've already been up in the attic. The ornaments and lights are ready to adorn him."

A slight shiver coursed down my spine, bringing me back to the present. My reminiscing and dreaming about Mother's beloved tree family further opened my mind to the world around me. I looked upward at the tall gray tree with its bare arms and hands.

If the others could walk and talk, how normal was it for this elderly lady to do the same?

"Wake up!" I shouted, tapping her darkened skin.

With the whistling wind blowing through her many arms, I could hear her wheezing and snoring. I yelled, jumping up and down on her red dress and feet.

"Talk to me again."

She awoke and groggily answered in a maple syrup voice. "What is it? I pointed you north. What more do you want of me?"

"Come with me to Mother's house," I said. "You needn't live and die alone out here."

The tree's arms crackled above me. "I'm too old to travel far. Don't know if I could make it. How distant is she?"

"At the end of that rainbow." I turned and pointed in the direction she'd suggested earlier. "In a valley with friends of yours. You'll see."

Her arms and body creaked. Little by little, she

pulled her feet free of the soil. She bent forward and extended a hand in my direction.

"Climb aboard, little man. I'll carry you to Mother. Then, maybe you'll let me sleep."

I grinned and reached out to curl my hands around one of her fingers. Pumping my legs, I pushed myself forward and slid across the palm of her hand. I sat down and made myself comfortable.

The tree straightened and gently curled her fingers around me. She took a swift turn and headed north.

"My pot of gold awaits," I said, eager to make it home to introduce Mother to her family and share the fortune with her.

Enjoy an excerpt from by Donald Kemp's humorous story, *Senior Touring Society.*

What could possibly go wrong with a group of gentle, lovable, and temperate seniors?

A seasoned, but often misunderstood group of seniors is determined in enjoying life to the fullest. Lost in the euphoria of the past while living in the present, the seniors make every day count. They get together every month to toss around ideas and decide on suitable trips that will broaden their horizons.

For you, the reader, some of their actions will make you laugh. Some will remind you of someone you know, making you think along the lines of, "Oh, yeah, that's just like my Uncle Harry!"

An eclectic bunch, the group often gets into trouble wherever they go. Nevertheless, the ensuing shenanigans don't deter them from their current goal—to make the most of the trips they take. From a stroll through a doctor's office, having tea, or spending time with friends and family, the seniors are there for one another whenever needed.

The Senior Touring Society is determined in providing as much entertainment for themselves as often as possible. Planning their trips is never easy, however. There are ups and downs, and all sorts of details to hammer out. Though the seniors often get more than they've bargained for, they're willing to make the best of the situations they find themselves in.

CHAPTER ONE

THE SENIOR TOURING SOCIETY MEETING

THE late Harrison Secord, one of the charter members of the Senior Touring Society, endowed enough money in his trust to purchase a small one-story building one block off Main Street. A section of the trust provides funds to pay for future taxes and upkeep. Originally a ladies dress shop, it shares common walls with shops on each side. Large windows can be seen along the front wall of the building once occupied by mannequins in fancy dresses.

A charter member who owns a furniture store has donated plenty of chairs and tables that can be arranged to the members' liking.

Another charter member volunteered to remove

the faded red and gold flowered wallpaper, repair any defects in the walls, and prepare them for painting, doing the work without labor costs and only charging for any materials used. The members have chosen a soft eggshell white color to help brighten the long, narrow room. The solid oak floors were sanded smooth and sealed with a long-lasting non-skid wax.

Several nicely framed photos of past trips adorn the walls. The back wall has a small closet that is used for the storage of the Society's tables, chairs, and the coffee urn. A few dishes and supplies to make the coffee can be found in a wall cabinet with a small sink below. A shelf holds coffee mugs with each member's name on the side. A door to the parking lot stands to the right of the closet. On the other side is a very small room with a commode and sink.

LYLE, an ex-army sergeant, retired with thirty-six years of service, joined the society four years ago when he turned fifty-five. He sports a brush haircut and always wears a black bow tie with a heavily starched white shirt.

Today is Tuesday. Some of the members have already arrived for the monthly meeting. Lyle is

SENIOR TOURING SOCIETY

always the first to open the front doors and make coffee in the urn. He has brought out a few chairs and a table for the chairperson.

"We really need a small fridge," he says to Sally, who is sipping her coffee nearby.

"At almost every meeting, we talk about that, but nobody has bought one."

"I'll see what some of the charities have for sale this week and get it. No sense in putting it off any longer."

"Need any help, Lyle? I would be happy to go with you. Maybe we could take in a movie and have dinner someplace romantic. We could talk about going to our island in the South Pacific."

"Thanks for the offer, Sally, but I can't do it. I'll probably go shopping on my lunch hour and not have time for a movie and dinner."

The Society meets at least once a month to plan and organize various day trips and tours for the coming months. A chairperson is assigned alphabetically for the monthly meetings, so no one person is stuck with the job for every meeting. A separate list is kept for the 'special' tours. The chairperson does the research for costs, accommodations, and other necessary items.

Today, Emma is in charge of the meeting about approving a trip for the annual 'special' tour, which can be as long as a week rather than just a day trip. She moves to the chairperson's table and sits down on the chair provided, her hands curled beneath her to keep them from trembling.

Lyle has become the self-appointed leader of the Senior Touring Society, acting as guardian and occasional problem solver on tours. Standing beside Emma, he places a gentle hand on her shoulder and whispers in her ear.

"I'm right beside you. You can do this. Stand tall. Turn around and face your friends."

Lyle smiles and nods at Emma. Being a chairperson for a special tour isn't easy for most of the members. Nevertheless, he has faith in her and knows she'll do what's best for the Society.

EMMA takes a deep breath in the hopes of stilling her racing heart. She dreads her turn as chairperson, or any other leadership position for the group. The chair position for the week-long tour has kept her awake several nights for the past month. When sleep finally came, her nightmares were filled with fearful incidences waking her up in a sweat.

Emma is the original *plain Jane* type. She is of average height, average weight, and average pretty. From top to toe, she is average everything. She still wears clothes she bought twenty years ago that show very little signs of wear. The small pink purse she carries was purchased at a bargain counter in a flea market along with several pairs of shoes with low heels. She has the same Dutch Boy haircut with bangs she wore in high school and never wears any make-up.

In high school, she was the shy wallflower. Now, fifty-two years later, Emma is the same almost invisible person. When she speaks, which is seldom, her voice is so low, you can barely hear the words.

Sitting on the chair in front of a small table, Emma's spine is straight and as stiff as a board. A few feet in front of her, two rows of chairs are arranged in a semi-circle.

She has delayed the start of the meeting, trying to find the courage to speak. Emma takes a deep breath and shifts in her seat, glancing at the members behind her. She realizes that no one is looking in her direction and slowly stands on wobbly feet. Her whole body shakes, though she does her best to tamp it down.

She leans closer to Lyle and whispers, "Don't leave me."

Lyle still has a hand on her shoulder. He gives it a little pat-pat for reassurance.

"I'm right beside you. You can do this. Stand tall. Turn around and face your friends."

RUN, she thinks.

The members are milling about in the front of the room and talking to each other. Most are munching on the homemade cookies and drinking coffee from their personal decorated mugs. The sixty-cup coffee urn is sitting on a table nearby with a plate of cookies. Now, only two remain.

With a nod of encouragement from Lyle, Emma takes another deep breath. Her voice squeaks when she speaks.

"Everyone, please come and sit down. We have to get this meeting started."

Several members look her way, but they don't move.

"Come on, everyone," she says once more with an uncertain tone. "Let's get the meeting started."

Ellen and Maggie slowly move toward the waiting chairs.

Ellen is petite, slim, five feet tall, and is still quite attractive, appearing much younger than her eighty years. She became a young widow when her first husband was killed in a terrible auto accident. Desperate for money, she secured a probationary job at the library of the local university. When she retired thirty-five years later, she was the "head cheese," as she calls it. Although mild in manner, she has a quick wit and often surprises everyone with her outlandish remarks.

"I hope we go to England, Maggie. I was there once, and it was so lovely."

As she passes by Lyle, he says, "I bet you met the Queen."

"If I had, I certainly would brag about it. But I

did see President Roosevelt's wife, Eleanor, once when she was in a parade. I was named after her, you know. I don't know if my mother ever saw her. She just named me Ellen."

"What does that have to do with the Queen of England?" Maggie asks.

Maggie, who is in her mid-nineties, is the eldest of the group. She is a little hard of hearing and refuses to get a hearing aid.

"I'm not old enough for one of those things," she often scoffs.

She carries a cane with elaborate gold and pearl inlays. Maggie is still agile enough that the cane is seldom used for balance. She carries it under her arm like a British Army officer. Sometimes, she'll hold it up in the air, waving it around like a drum majorette.

"What did she say?" Maggie asks, leaning toward Ellen to hear the answer.

"Who?"

"The Queen. What did the Queen say?"

"I didn't meet the Queen."

"I heard Lyle say you met the Queen."

"You would need very special connections to meet the Queen of England."

"If you didn't, you should have." Maggie bangs her cane hard on the floor. She slowly drifts apart from Ellen, muttering under her breath. "I wouldn't go all the way to England and not see the Queen. Who would spend all that money to go to England and not see the Queen? Some people are just . . . well, just . . ."

"Okay, everyone, quiet down," Emma says in a soft tone. She continues trying to get the members seated and the meeting started. "Find a chair. We need to get started."

"Louder," someone shouts.

Lyle stands by her side and says, "You're doing fine." He raises an open hand, gesturing for her to raise her voice.

She tilts her head at him and nods.

"Okay, I'll try." Emma takes another deep breath. "Lyle is ready to tell us about our next special annual tour. Sit down, everyone."

Her tone of voice rises with a little more confidence. She glances at Lyle and smiles.

He bends down and grabs the gavel lying on the table, pounding it several times across its surface.

Without a word, the seniors glance at him, and then hasten to find a seat. Several chairs scrape across the oak floor. Lyle's intense scrutiny causes them to hurry. Soft murmurs can be heard amongst them before the silence descends.

"As I said, Lyle is ready to tell us about the new special trip for this year. Lyle, your turn."

She gestures with an open hand for him to continue and immediately sits down, relieved that her part may be over for the day. *Thank heaven I don't have to do this again until next year.*

"That's better." Lyle pauses. In a gentler voice, he says, "Our next long tour may need more than one week to see everything. I have been searching online for more than two weeks for a nice tour. I went to several travel agencies and found an island with fantastic nightlife, beautiful art and museums, exotic food, scenery as far as your eye can see, mountains, and waterfalls."

"A little less bally-hoo," Maude cries in a loud voice. "Tell us where we're going."

Maude is nearing her seventy-second birthday and has always been in control of her family affairs. She tries to exert control over every situation she encounters, family or otherwise. Some people—behind her back, of course—whisper that she carries a bullwhip hidden within her clothing.

She buys almost all her clothes at yard sales. Most do not fit her rather stout figure. Today, she is wearing a faded red blouse with a pair of green hospital ER scrubs. White shoes and a flowered wide brim hat that has a purple feather attached to one side complete the ensemble.

"I bet it's a tropical island in the South Pacific," Sally whispers to Lotie, who is sitting beside her. "Palm trees and snow white beaches. Lyle and I can lie on the warm sand all day and night, content to just be with each other."

Sally turned sixty-five a month ago. She often lets her thoughts wander off to some dream association with Lyle. Sometimes, she gets so lost in her dream world that she wanders away from the group, forcing Lyle to search for her without losing track of the other seniors. Lost in her thoughts, Sally is oblivious to the meeting and continues to talk aloud.

"I know that someday we will find a nice deserted South Pacific island and live the rest of our lives in total bliss. Maybe have someone to help around the house, but I will do the cooking. Lyle won't have to do anything, maybe fish. He loves to fish."

"Wake up, Sally," Maude says. "You're daydreaming about you and Lyle again. It's not going to happen." She faces Emma and Lyle, shouting in her usual loud voice. "Hey, Lyle. How much is this dream tour going to cost?"

"This tour would be cheap at half the cost."

"I don't like the sound of this." Helga stands. "Anything that sounds cheap usually is cheap."

Helga has celebrated her thirty-ninth birthday at least thirty-nine times. She hears only what she wants to hear, and then erupts into outbursts, orating as if she's on a soapbox, not caring if anyone is listening or not.

Most of the seniors ignore her rants and turn away.

Helga never seems to mind that she has lost her audience. Most people wonder if she ever takes her faded green pillbox hat off. The joke amongst the seniors is she wears it to bed. A rather hefty woman, Helga is not as well off as the other seniors. She often struggles to make ends meet. To make up for her shortage of funds, she strives to put on a show of

SENIOR TOURING SOCIETY

indignation over most things.

"I can tell you horror stories about cheap. My first husband was cheap." Helga folds her arms across her chest and sits down. "Thank heaven I got rid of him. That old skinflint was worthless."

"Have faith, everyone," Lyle says. "You will talk about this tour for the rest of your lives."

"If you don't tell us where this tour is going soon, we'll all be dead," Maude shouts.

A murmuring of voices ripples throughout the room. Several heads nod in agreement.

"Maybe he doesn't know how old we are," Helga snickers.

The murmuring grows a little louder.

Lyle clears his throat to gain the group's attention once more. "Okay, here it is, ladies." He holds up a book titled, *Iceland In A Nut Shell*. "We're going to Iceland."

A thick, uneasy silence descends upon the group. Then, everyone speaks at once.

"Iceland? Who wants to go there?"

"Did he say Iceland?"

"Where is that?"

"I heard they don't like Americans."

"That's nothing strange."

"I don't have a winter coat."

"Who wants to spend a wad of money just to see a bunch of igloos and Eskimos?"

"We'll probably have to eat whale blubber the entire time we are there."

Helga stands up and tramps toward the door. "This meeting is a waste of my time. Who in hell wants to go there? I'm going home."

Victoria whispers, "You shouldn't say that 'h' word in mixed company, Helga."

"What? Hell? They say it in church, so I can say it here."

"What a rip-off," Maude exclaims in disgust. "Iceland. Phooey, I'm going home, too."

Chairs scrape across the floor once more. The members turn and talk to each other. Some prepare to leave.

Emma stands, intent on calming everyone down. She surprises herself by calling out to them in a loud voice.

"Wait, wait. Please sit back down. Helga, Maude, please, Lyle has more to tell us."

Lyle pounds the gavel again.

"ORDER!" Emma shouts, sinking back down onto her chair.

I just shouted. How did I do that?

Maude and Helga, surprised by Emma's unusual outburst, obey and sit down. They look around, sheepish grins spreading across their faces.

The rest of the members return the chairs to their previous places and sit down.

Emma stares straight ahead, full of confusion. *I shouted*, she thinks. *Everyone listened to me.*

"Okay, ladies," Lyle says, speaking in a soft voice. "How about a warm water natural spring that leaves your skin as soft as a baby's behind?" He tilts his head up and closes his eyes, gently caressing his raised arms. "Mmmm, so soft."

Victoria interrupts the moment. She is the typical "prim and proper" person, almost seventy-five years old, and widowed over twenty-five years ago. Her husband took care of everything for her, so she doesn't understand much of what is going on.

She carries a flask and takes what she thinks are secret little sips. Unfortunately, her rather slight frame doesn't allow her to drink much of the bourbon before she grows tipsy. Her expensive clothes become disheveled long before any tour is over. Her steps grow wobbly and the prim and proper appearance flies out the window.

"Do they have stores so I can get my special medicine? Will they be able to fill my medicine bottle? I need refills almost every day." Victoria shifts in her chair, turning her back to everyone, pretending to cough while taking a sip from her flask.

Maggie ignores Victoria and turns her attention to Ellen. "I thought we were going to Angel Falls. I never got to go there. We lived right on the corner of Hickory Falls Road and Clairmont Road. All we had to do was drive east down Angel Falls Road, and it would be right there in front of us, but we never did."

"I thought you said you lived on Angel Falls Road?" Ellen asks.

"Some called it Hickory Falls Road, and others, Angel Falls. I liked Angel Falls better."

"Is Angel Falls on an island?" Sally asks.

Maggie ponders the question. "No, I don't think so. Of course, we never went, so it could be, I guess. They say it's just a few miles east of our farm. You can't miss it because Angel Falls Road is a dead end."

"I went to Niagara Falls once with my sister," Ellen says. "We took the train from Windsor. I saw both sides, the American and the Canadian."

"I'm looking for a nice quiet island for Lyle and me to lie on the beach all day," Sally states. "We will have someone to help around the house, too."

Ellen looks in her direction, shaking her head, somewhat in pity and somewhat annoyed. "Sally, you always talk about a deserted island with Lyle that is never going to happen. Why don't you and I go for a vacation somewhere?"

"Oh, I don't think I could without Lyle. Could we ask him to go with us?"

A quiet sigh slips past Sally's lips. She closes her eyes and loses herself in her thoughts of a romance with Lyle, ignoring Ellen's remark, oblivious to where she is.

"Never give up your dream, girl. It will happen someday, me and Lyle on the beach with a gentle breeze off the ocean," she murmurs.

"Everyone, please listen to Lyle," Lotie adds. "I've been to Iceland twice, and it is beautiful. This will be a tour you will tell your grandchildren about, and your great grandchildren, too."

Lotie is only seventy-three years of age, but she

still goes to all the local nightspots, church socials, and bingo games. She is always on the lookout for a new man in her life.

She lowers her voice, whispering to Ellen. "Maybe this time I could meet a nice Icelandic lad, eh?"

Helga stands up and grunts with disgust. "Humph! We'll all be dead before that happens if this stupid meeting goes on any longer." Her chair makes a loud grinding noise as she drops onto her seat in a forceful manner.

"I think we should vote on it," Victoria offers. "My Herbert always said we should vote on things."

Emma tries to restore order, but her loud voice has escaped her. She turns to Lyle with pleading eyes.

"Do something, Lyle."

"It's your meeting, Emma. I told them what I thought would be a nice place to go. Now, I might suggest somewhere else."

Emma stands up. Her fingers are wrapped around the gavel, though she forgets to use it.

"Does everyone have a passport? We will all need passports. They are real easy to get. You need your birth certificate and a special sized photo—"

"That does it," Maude says, and stands. "No one takes my picture." She waves her hand in the air. "No one." She turns and walks toward the rear door.

Ellen leans toward Maggie. "I wonder why she doesn't want her picture taken."

"Because she is wanted in twenty-nine states,

that's why," Helga says, laughing at her own joke.

"Really? I didn't know that," Ellen replies. "I can't imagine anybody being wanted in twenty-nine states. I wonder what she did."

The seniors are all standing now and saying their goodbyes. None of them are paying attention to Emma.

She sits down, her shoulders slumped, head bowed. A deep groan slides past her lips.

"Phooey," she says. "I quit."

Lyle places a soft hand on Emma's shoulder. He slowly walks away without saying a word.

Be sure to check out Donald Kemp's debut novel, *Rendering*, published by Alegos Press.

Immerse yourselves in a world where . . .

Nothing is ever as it seems.

Ted Monroe's life changes in the blink of an eye. Privy to a fatal airplane crash, his job as a pilot ends several days later. When the NSA shows up on his very doorstep, Ted begins to wonder what he's gotten himself into. A suspected smuggling ring has been found in a small southwestern town. It's up to him to find out as much as possible about it in the hopes of bringing it to an end.

Out of work and hoping for a better tomorrow, Ted leaves Michigan, hoping to find something that will give his life meaning once more. Deep inside, he knows he should walk away. Unfortunately, he has no other choice but to do as the NSA demands. If he's to succeed in doing exactly as they ask, he'll have to put all of his acquired pilot skills to good use.

Determined to follow through with the orders he's been given, Ted soon sets foot in Cartia. The town looks like just like any other town, though appearances can sometimes be deceiving. When attempts on his life are made, he soon realizes he may be in way over his head. He'll have to dig deep to get to the bottom of things if he's to survive unscathed.

ABOUT THE AUTHOR

Donald Kemp was born and raised in Southern Michigan and lived in North Carolina for over thirty-six years, and thus, is no longer a damn Yankee. He graduated from a combination of high school and aircraft mechanics school. Two years later, he became the supervisor for one of the Michigan National Guard Air Section Maintenance shops. He married his beautiful wife, Gerry, and has three children, eight grandchildren, and nine great-grandchildren.

Serious writing began with thirteen weekly articles in the Rochester City newspaper about his heart bypass surgery in the very early days of the procedure at Cleveland Clinic. Donald later published the book, *I Live With A Mended Heart*, and distributed it to doctors and hospitals all over the United States.

Donald wrote and directed three stage plays for a senior acting group in Southern California. He has also written numerous short stories about his relatives' blips and/or accomplishments for the family archives. Several children's books will be ready soon for publishing. Nowadays, airplanes, helicopters, furniture building, and consulting for interior decorators have given way to writing novels and short stories based on his varied life adventures. His novel, *Rendering*, was published in April 2016 by Alegos Press.